A HEART IN TWO CITIES

I0608269

by

ANGELA PEACH
and
S J CAMPBELL

A CIP catalogue record for this title is available from the British library.

Cover Art — Marcus Marritt Illustrator

Published by RingeAlba Books.

ISBN 978-0-9932535-7-7

Sometimes, looking up at the clouds passing by overhead would make me so dizzy I'd have to close my eyes and hold my breath until the feeling receded to a manageable level. Today was one of those days, but the unsteadiness refused to ease off and I knew I was going to struggle to pull myself out of this particular funk.

With a heavy sigh, I pushed myself up from the ground I was laying on and rested my head on my knees. I felt so confused, unsure of how to feel or handle my emotions or even the situation. I mean, for one thing I wasn't sure whether to walk across the graveyard and join the funeral or not. Would I even be welcomed? If I blamed myself for her death, surely the rest of her family would too? I wouldn't forget the look her mother had given me in the hospital in a hurry, that was for sure.

I rubbed my face hard, wondering if I should be crying. So fucking confused. Don't get me wrong, I of all people, was used to feeling confused. It was so normal for me now that, well, it *was* normal! But this was something I'd never thought would happen and there weren't even any support groups available because I'd checked. I suppose not many people got killed on a first date.

And I'd really liked her, too. Her name had been Poppy and she'd had the darkest eyes I'd ever seen. She'd had kind of an old style gypsy look about her, as if she should be peering knowingly into a crystal ball to tell you your future. Although if that had been the case I'm pretty sure she would have run as far away from me as possible. As *quickly* as possible.

I'd been really looking forward to getting to know her better. And yes, that translated into 'I'd been looking forward to shagging her brains out' just as much and I didn't care if that made me shallow.

I played with the unopened pack of cigarettes in my hand, contemplating having one although I'd never smoked before (well, in a way I suppose I sort of had...no, I didn't want to think about *her* today because Poppy deserved all of my attention) I knew though, that if I tried to smoke one of these, I'd probably end up hacking and hawking my guts up, but I just felt like it was the right time to finally have one. As a trickle of sweat rolled down the side of my face, I sighed again. Poor Poppy, the cowgirl from Ohio with the dark eyes and the sexy come to bed smile.

I lay back down and closed my eyes to block out the sun and the world.

*** *** ***

It was nearly an hour later before I 'woke' sitting up and staring at my surroundings in puzzlement, making sure I was still this 'me' before relaxing. You see, I don't sleep or dream, so getting lost in my thoughts with my eyes closed was the closest I got to being asleep. But I always had to check where I was carefully when I did 'wake up' to make sure I knew who I was.

The Arkansas sky was a deep azure blue and I gazed up at it smiling before I remembered where I was and why I was there. The funeral was bound to have come to an end by now, so I got to my feet and brushed the dust and dirt from my new black pants (bought specially for today) before shakily and hesitantly walking down the hill, keeping my eyes alert for any of Poppy's friends and family. To be honest, even if they didn't blame me, I couldn't bear to see their pain and tears and anguish that I had ultimately been the root cause of.

My cell ringing in my pocket shook me from my thoughts and I debated letting it go to answer phone, but I'm just too damn nosey to not at least see who it was calling, so I fished it out, instantly glad I had.

"Hey mom, you ok?"

"Of course I am, Nikki honey, I was just calling to see how you were holding up. Did you go in the end?"

Mom had known the turmoil I'd been experiencing about whether or not to attend Poppy's funeral and told me to just follow my heart. I ran a hand through my short red hair, looking up at the sky again.

"Kinda. I came, but I just stayed out of the way."

"I thought you would. So will you be back for dinner?"

"I'll be home soon, but I'm not hungry so don't keep me anything." I knew she would anyway. Just in case.

"Ok, sweetie. Well, I'll see you soon then. Ride carefully?"

"Always do. Love you mom."

"Love you too."

We hung up and I realised I'd managed to get to Poppy's final resting place, currently a nasty brown gash in the ground waiting to be filled in properly. Everything seemed very surreal all of a sudden — the baking hot sun refused to penetrate the chill surrounding me and the air became heavy and hard to draw into my lungs.

"Oh, Poppy. I'm so sorry." I whispered, feeling tears well in my eyes. But they were selfish tears born of guilt and regret and I refused to let them fall. Because despite barely knowing the girl, currently residing six feet below me, I'd definitely wanted to get to know her. We'd started out so well with so much promise.

"Oh. It's you."

I think I may have cringed, even as I jumped. I recognised the voice before I saw the owner and I don't really know why I was so surprised that she was still here when everyone else had gone on to the wake. Poppy had been really close to her sister, Malena, who, apart from looking at me with what seemed like barely concealed hatred, had been the only family member that had spoken to me at the hospital.

"Hi."

We stood awkwardly for a minute, not knowing what to say. I mean, what could we say? I noted that her dark eyes, not so dissimilar from her sister's, were dry and wondered how she'd managed to hold herself together. Then the thought occurred to me that maybe she'd been saving them for a private moment. Like now.

"Uh...I'd better make a move. I'm sorry." I started turning to walk away but she grabbed my arm.

"Wait! Nikki, please stay a while longer? I thought I wanted to be alone..." she trailed off but the evident desperation was something I couldn't ignore. For some bizarre reason I felt if I said that my mom was waiting for me to come home it would grind salt into her wound.

"Ok."

Her shoulders sagged in relief, but then we seemed stuck on looking awkwardly at each other not knowing what to say. I frantically rummaged my muddled mind.

"The doctors said...they said she didn't suffer, y'know cos...I mean, you were there with her...did...did she?" Malena stuttered, her voice choking off to a whisper at the end. I shook my head vehemently.

"No! It was all so quick, but I'm pretty sure she didn't...you know."

"She didn't deserve to die. She had so many plans. She was supposed to...oh God, I think I need to sit down."

She kind of fell down in a strange crumpled manner and I rushed to her side.

"Can I get you anything?" It was a stupid question because obviously there was only one thing she needed.

"A cigarette? I'd really like a smoke if you've got one?"

I berated myself for feeling stupidly pleased that I had exactly what she had asked for, fumbling with the wrapper to open it and pass her one. Maybe I should always carry a pack around, like an alternative first aid kit. I noticed both our hands were shaking as I struck a match and she had to hold mine with her own in order for the flame to make contact. Then she looked so content after taking a really deep drag that I pulled one out for myself, hoping I wasn't going to look stupid. Malena hurried to help hold my hands steady when I lit the match and I made eye contact with her.

Thank you.

She gave the briefest of smiles.

You're welcome.

Then I had a spectacular coughing fit as the alien smoke hit my lungs and was rejected immediately.

"Shit, are you ok?"

I nodded, waving one of my hands to dismiss her worry.

"Fine...just..." A fresh wave of coughs hit and I could feel my face getting redder and redder, not just with the exertion but with embarrassment too.

"Not had one for a while, huh?"

I managed to get some modicum of control back and shook my head. "No. Don't even know why I started in the first place. Or why I bought these." I held the pack out to her. "You can have them if you want?"

"Thanks. Although if I'm perfectly honest, I gave up a few years ago. I just felt like one ever since..." Her jaw moved, so she put the cigarette in and took another deep drag. I regarded mine and decided to butt it out on the ground rather than risk further choking, but because it felt wrong to be leaving it on the ground, I kept hold of it in my clammy hand. A plane flew overhead and we both looked up to watch it, glad of the diversion.

"When I was younger, I thought the clouds were the souls of dead people floating around in the sky. I thought that the rain was the dead souls way of crying on us, sobbing and wishing they could come back, but because it was always so sunny and cloudless here, that this was a good place to live and die. I thought here was better than there, in the UK, cos it always rains there."

My outburst surprised even me, and I wished I could take it all back. I wished I could find solace in the drag of a cigarette. I wished I could just get away with running back to the car park, gunning up my bike and getting the fuck out of this town as if I had the devil on my tail. I was opening my mouth to apologise when she spoke.

"Would...would you like to go for a drink?"

I stared at her in shock — that was definitely not the reaction I'd expected.

"I don't think I'd be very welcome," I mumbled, trying to stuff my hands into pockets that just weren't in these pants.

"I didn't mean the wake. I meant would you like to come to a dirty bar and get blind steamin' drunk with me? I don't think I can handle the whole family thing, y'know? Please?"

"Uh...sure. But I've got my bike with me..."

"That's ok, I can ride with you. I'll pay for a cab to get you home," she added, almost desperately.

"Ok, I'll come...but you don't need to pay for my cab." With that we both fell silent again.

It was another hour before we both walked with heavy legs back to my Ducati Monster, stood proud and alone in the cool shadow of a tree waiting for me. I unlocked my helmet and handed it to her while I got Monster fired up. I'd had her for nearly two years now, but the sound of her purring still pleased me. Malena seemed suitably impressed although she looked like she was struggling with the chin strap. I beckoned her to me so I could tighten it, ignoring her breasts pushing against my elbow.

"Make sure you hold on tight, ok? I mean *real* tight." She nodded, and I hoped she understood the importance of this instruction. My bike was fast, and even though I wasn't planning on opening her up, she was still pretty lethal. "And lean with me when we go round corners — it'll make it easier for me."

"I know. My ex had a bike, but it wasn't as nice as this one."

She swung her leg up and over, sitting snug against me and wrapping her arms around me tight before I twisted the throttle and headed for the bar we'd agreed on during the walk back. It was in the next town, which suited us both just fine — I don't think either of us was in the mood to bump into anyone we knew.

The bar was indeed dirty and the sort of dive I'd normally feel uncomfortable just walking by in broad daylight. But we weren't really in the mood to care and we walked on through the front entrance like we were regulars, ignoring the stares from all the actual regulars. At the bar, she ordered some shots of Wild Turkey, telling the barman to "Keep 'em comin'" which he did very successfully.

There are moments in your life which stand out as being huge, *big* mistakes and you are fully aware of this even as you willingly do whatever it is you are doing, but you do it anyway.

That was how I felt when Malena and I ended up in a cheap, dirty motel quite a few hours later, tearing at each other's clothes angrily while our mouths smashed together in a lustful embrace.

I'd deal with the consequences tomorrow.

CHAPTER TWO

I came to with my tongue stuck to the roof of my mouth, my lips cracking dry and a shiver beginning to work its way up my body. I had kicked the sheets off in my slumber again, forever fighting invisible demons in my dreamless sleep. I reluctantly dragged my body from the mattress, flicking on the one-bar heater on my way to the kitchen area where my kettle lived.

I leant against the units as I waited for the boil, one arm wrapped across my stomach, the other rubbing my head. I'd drunk too much again the night before it would seem.

I looked around my apartment — bed in the far corner, door off to the bathroom, an old two-seater at one wall and in front of my large windows stood my canvas.

My empty canvas.

I made my tea and sat sipping cross-legged on the couch, staring at the blank canvas, as the sun shone in, illuminating the dust in the air, moving endlessly.

This is all I have to show for my life: a flat I can barely afford and only enough clean pants to get me through a week. My life could have been so different and, as always moments after waking, my thoughts turned to Helena. I thought of her smile and how it illuminated my life like a sun, bringing warmth and a heat inside me. I thought of the touch of her fingers, tracing designs on my skin and how I longed to feel her body on mine once more.

At sixteen, Helena had walked into my classroom and sat beside me, as she always did. We had been best friends since our very first day at Primary School. She leant over and whispered to me, "David has asked me to the school dance."

I felt my face redden with fury. I had the temper to go with my fiery hair. "What did you say?"

She laughed, tossing her long, curly brown hair over her shoulders in a move that froze me with its eroticism. My belly button danced, as I gulped down my yearning. "I told him no, of course, Nick." Then she leant in even closer, "You know I only have eyes for you."

I shivered, not knowing how I would get through the rest of the day, until I could hold her in my arms, feeling the pressure of her breasts on mine and kiss her.

She moved back, smiling at the effect she knew she had on me, leaving her leg touching mine. I would die of anticipation. We had been lovers for years by then, even at that tender age. When Helena wanted something, there was no-one who could stand in her way and Helena wanted me. I let her have me, powerless to resist her mesmerising dark eyes and I loved her with all of my heart.

I would love her forever, too.

I never knew how good love could be until I could no longer hold it, like sand slipping through my fingers.

As my thoughts followed the familiar road to darkness, I got up to look for my cigarettes, finding a crumpled pack of 'Marlboros' under my discarded jumper. I pulled the jumper on over the top of my vest, wandering over to the gas cooker, the jumper covering my pants, leaving my legs bare. I clicked on a ring, carefully bending down to light my smoke without singeing my hair.

I inhaled, ready to face the painful memories with the assistance of nicotine.

Oh my darling, Helena, my reason for existing.

The old anger rushed up, taking me by surprise and I slid down my kitchen units, bringing my knees up to my face, curling into a ball. It didn't stop the pain reaching in and clenching an ice cold fist around my heart, squeezing the happiness from my life.

"I could have loved you," I said to no-one. But always to Helena.

It's no good how this misery creeps up on me at every opportunity, a snake that winds its way up my legs and across my stomach, laying a weight on my chest. I have enough darkness in my life without the black of love throwing itself over me, like a blinding cape.

I took the last drag of my fag and threw it in the sink, running the tap a few seconds. I found the packet to light another but it was empty. I groaned because now I would have to go out.

Over at my bed, I slipped on the jeans and socks I'd thrown in a corner and stood into some scuffed boots, not bothering to lace them. I had a washed out coffee jar that I kept my change in and I turned it upside-down, the coins rattling on the work surface. I have been reduced to counting pennies to buy myself some cigarettes.

On my eighteenth birthday, Helena had given me a delicately wrapped box and I had been afraid to open it.

"What is it?" I had asked, with a tremble in my voice.

"Open it and see, silly," she had smiled.

My fingers shook and I pulled off the paper. A box.

"A box," I said.

"You are a box," she said, kissing me.

I opened the box and saw two beautiful diamond stud earrings. Helena's mum and dad had plenty of money and she was never afraid to spend it.

"They're gorgeous," I said, the breath whipped from me.

"Put them on." A whisper here and there in memory.

I still have them in their box. I could sell them and get a few hundred quid but that would feel like I was giving up and I would never give up on Helena. She said I was like a box but she was wrong: a box has six sides and I only have three.

I slammed shut my front door and made my way downstairs, hoping to avoid Freya, the cheerful Norwegian who lived below me but it was not to be. Her door opened as I reached it, her Nordic sixth sense grinning at me.

"Hello! You must come for dinner tonight."

"I must?"

"Oh, you must," she smiled, her eyes sparkling with a hint of mischievousness. "Tonight, seven, I will cook. You need fattening."

I need flattering, not fattening, I thought.

"Yes, yes," I said, skipping away and escaping to the street, where I could walk and feel the cold slap of the wind on my face, while the sun shone tempting me to remain outdoors. I was only trying to sneak out for some ciggies and there was Freya, never one to miss a chance to ambush me.

I thought of her blue eyes and her ice white hair that sloped down her back like a ski piste, over her broad shoulders. Strong, broad shoulders that held up a most luscious pair of pert breasts and a smile that teased with a pair of dimpled cheeks. I could find worse distractions.

She left me alone on my way back in, now that I had agreed to let her feed me but, let's face it, beggars can't be choosers and I was practically a beggar. Opening my fridge to a mouldy lump of cheese confirmed that but all was not lost, as I saw the four pack of lager. That would do nicely.

My phone rang. I saw from caller-display that it was my mum.

"What?" I said.

"Hi, Nick, honey, do you want to come over for dinner tonight?"

"Freya's cooking for me."

"Freya?" I heard the surprise and hope in her voice.

"Yes. Freya. Her downstairs."

"You have a lovely time, sweetheart."

"Humph," I muttered, hanging up. She would love to see me with someone else, someone who could take my mind off Helena.

I remembered my mum's gentle words. "It's been a year now, Nick honey, you need to move on." I still heard them, years later, whistling around my vacant room.

"You need to move on." Never!

I lit my cigarette, throwing the wrapping paper into the sink and, as I inhaled, I looked at my canvas waiting to be touched by colours. Every day is an empty canvas, waiting for the lines and colours to lead the way.

I threw off my jumper, back to the corner I had found it and stood in front of my canvas, the sun hitting my face from the windows behind. I saw in my mind the day that Helena had stood in front of my windows, posing, for me to paint her. She wore a red dress, thin straps over her shoulders holding a hugging velvet that draped around her feet like a pool of blood and that held her curves to it, her breasts edging their beginnings.

I swallowed down my heart in my throat as I closed my eyes, overcome by the beauty of her ghostly presence. If I reached out my hand would surely touch her... I would surely feel her under my fingers... I could bring her close to me once more.

I opened my eyes and there was nothing. There is always nothing when I dare myself to look. I grabbed my palette, mixing paints with my brush, dabbing out the water, as my eyes began to see the shapes of emotion that I needed to get out. Only painting would release my tears and my doubts; only throwing the brush across the canvas could calm me and give me hope for my future.

A future that lay with Helena.

Monsoons of colour materialised before me, mirroring the feelings in my mind. When I looked in a mirror, the eyes of a stranger looked back at me. I might die a struggling, penniless artist but I would be true to myself. And being true to myself meant being true to Helena.

I don't know how long I stood throwing colour on top of colour, swishing and swirling my paint brush, as if that could take the emotions from me and put them out for all to see. I would love to take my pain and paint it away, but then, what would I have left?

I looked over the canvas, to my wall of windows and saw the last light of the day. For a moment I stood, watching how the clouds ran after each other, never catching and thought how love was similar: I have run after love for years now and all I have to show is a sky full of clouds.

Washing my hands, I eyed the new pack of 'Marlboros' and lit one as soon as my hands were dry. I felt a calmness and scrolled through the numbers in my phone until I came to what I was looking for, pressing dial.

"Hello, George Chan speaking."

"Mr Chan, it's Nick."

"Ah, Nick. How are you?"

"Never mind how I am. Do you have any news for me?" For weeks I had been paying this Mr Chan to trace Helena for me and so far, he had come up with nothing but promises and fresh air.

"Two minutes," he said and I heard some shuffling of papers. "You want Helena X? I find. Have address."

I gasped. I never truly believed he would actually find her. It was just one more road for me to wander down with my dreams until I hit the usual dead-end. "You found her?"

"Oh, yes."

"Where is she?"

"You pay bill first."

I clenched my teeth. "I'll come in tomorrow and square up. It might be the day after. As soon as I can anyway." I hung up. I lit another cigarette, my heart battering my rib-cage, desperate to be close to its mate again.

"Be still," I whispered.

I went to my fridge, finding the lager and quickly opened a can, gulping down half. My heart was finding its regular beat but my mind still raced.

Oh, glorious Helena, once more within reach. I would savour this and lock myself into my daydreams for hours, seeing our meeting, the embrace, the kiss, the love-making. I could go over and over it, a million times, getting perfect my words of delight.

But first, I had a dinner with Freya.

An hour later, I trotted downstairs, freshly showered in a clean vest but the same jeans, holding my remaining two cans of lager. She opened her door quickly, likely having heard my footsteps above her, and she smiled.

"*Vakker kjaerlighet,*" I heard but I was staring into her smiling blue eyes, lagoons to drown in. Her hair lay in one simple, white braid, curling around her neck over her left shoulder, resting on her breast. She wore a white dress, peppered with bluebells, snug at the waist.

"Beautiful love," I whispered under my breath, with feelings that had been stolen from some other place. Another mind was finding mine.

"Come in, please. Our food is ready." In the face of such beauty, I felt worthless and almost turned on my heels like the coward I am, but her arm was softly on mine, leading me in and I had to obey.

We ate and chatted, drinking chilled white wine, with quiet music filling the gaps. When she laughed, she was the prettiest girl in the world.

After the umpteenth refill, Freya sat next to me on her settee, so close that I could smell the soap on her skin. It had been years since I looked into the eyes of a woman and felt an emotion akin to passion.

"I know you desire me, Nick," she breathed, closing in on me.

I *did* desire her.

I took her chin in my hand and pulled her to me, parting my lips in anticipation. I saw her eyes flutter shut as her lips met mine and my heart did that old familiar dance behind my breast.

And then Time stood still. For one singular second. There was no hammering in my head, or thudding in my temple, no sadness crawling over me and no dark cloud ready to rain.

Because she kissed me.

I put my hand to her breast, squeezing hard and I felt her tremble. We looked into each others eyes, centimetres apart, and then we kissed again, as I pushed myself closer to her. I felt her tug at my vest to get me nearer her, as our tongues felt shyly around the others.

And then I remembered Helena.

I pulled back, looking away guiltily.

"What's wrong?" she asked, trying to turn my face back to hers.

"I can't," I said. "I can't."

"Nick, your broken heart can heal. I am your medicine."

I gulped down a rising panic and let myself be embraced by Freya, her small frame surprisingly strong as she held me hard.

If I forgot Helena, she would be lost and if Helena was lost, then I would be lost. I would have lost myself then.

CHAPTER THREE

I woke up next to a warm body, a different warm body to that which I'd gone to bed with, and instantly groaned as the memory came rushing back. Typical. Trust Nick to make every effort to continue making a mess of her life. I always wondered if it was her way of saying 'Fuck you and your perfect world — deal with your own problems.' As if it was my fault her life was so fucked up.

Malena opened her eyes and I saw them focus on me in confusion as she processed the events of last night. Then, in an almost comical fashion, she recoiled away from me and jumped to her feet, taking the bed-sheet with her and holding it in belated modesty. I knew this routine so well that I believed I could say her lines for her before she got there herself, so I decided to save her the trouble.

"Look, we were both very drunk and very emotional so let's say we just forget this ever happened, ok?"

"You...you seduced me...you..."

"Whoa, hold up a second, you kissed me first in the toilets. Hell, you followed me in and locked the door behind us, so don't go pulling that crap on me," I interrupted, jumping out of the other side of the bed. She stared at me, obviously remembering how she'd thrown me into the cubicle back at the seedy bar, begging me to fuck her. I felt so sorry for her then that I nearly moved forward to placate the situation, but I inched backward instead.

"Now I'm gonna go take a shower which will give you enough time to get dressed and make your hasty exit. This will go no further than the two of us and we don't ever have to see each other again, ok? So just relax, give me a second, then you can go." Realising I was stark naked, I blushed and went quickly into the tiny bathroom, locking the door behind me (very unnecessary, but old habits and all that) before turning on the water. I cursed myself for behaving like a guy and not just saying no when a hot girl threw herself at me. It's not like I was so desperate for sex that I couldn't afford to turn her down gently. I felt a certain amount of smug satisfaction that I wasn't the only one making mistakes like that today — Nick was going to have to deal with Freya when *she* woke up.

The pitiful trickle of water did nothing for the hangover that was starting to seep through, but was enough to refresh me awake. It was only a short walk back to the bar to retrieve my bike and I decided I was ok to ride home, so long as I took it steady.

I gave myself a quick basic wash, but I was really only staying in the shower long enough to give Malena time to dress and disappear as fast as her straight, scared little legs could carry her. Ten minutes should definitely do it, I thought.

However, on exiting the bathroom I stopped in shock. Malena was stood in almost exactly the same position as when I'd left her, although she was now dressed and staring at me with uncertainty.

"I know it wasn't you. You know, last night. I can remember what happened, and it was...I just didn't want you to think...ah heck, Nikki, I don't know." Her bottom lip started to tremble, and I hesitated. I was wearing a scratchy small towel, but let's face it — she'd already seen everything I had in very intimate detail. I slowly moved across the short distance to her, wary in case she backed away. She didn't, and ended up kind of dissolving in my arms, burying her face in my neck as her tears finally fell. I held her, soothing her as best I could before guiding her to sit next to me on the bed. I wished I could summon up some tears of my own, but my eyes remained dry. Finally, she spoke in a husky, hushed voice.

"I had a strange dream last night. I was in this huge dark house and I went up to the attic to look for Poppy, but she wasn't there. And when I came back down the stairs, all the doors that had been open on the way up were now closed, and I could hear whispering behind them all, so I ran. But then there was this cold breeze behind me, like a hand, so I ran faster. When I made it downstairs, I had this thought that she was behind one of those doors and I went to go back in to look for her, but I was too scared. So I left her. I left her!"

"You didn't leave her, Malena. It was just a dream." I was a fine one to talk — I'd never had a single dream my whole life! I'd never experienced that terror of being chased, or the elation from flying that others got so excited about when re-telling the next day. Whereas most people took on a bored expression at the mere words 'I had the strangest dream last night...' I couldn't get enough of hearing about them! When I told them it was because I myself had never dreamed a dream, they usually said things like 'Oh, maybe you just don't remember them?' and I ended up agreeing with them simply because it was easier than offering up the real reason.

"Where do you think she is? Daddy thinks she's gone to hell for being a dyke...oh! I'm sorry, I didn't even think!" She looked horrified at her slip and I rushed to reassure her.

"It's ok, I've been called a lot worse! You didn't offend me."

"I just...what am I gonna do? I don't understand how I'm supposed to get through to the end of each day with this pain!" She squeezed her eyes shut and sagged, her fingers clutching painfully into my side. I stroked her hair, knowing there was nothing I could say.

Eventually, she managed to stem the flow of tears long enough to tug her mobile phone out of her pocket to call a cab. I didn't offer to give her a ride and she didn't ask for one.

As she left, she stopped by the door and turned to me.

"I don't regret what happened, Nikki. I'm grateful for last night, crazy as that sounds."

"No, I get it." And I did, in a weird sort of way. I'd been a distraction from being around a family suffering in pain, from distant relatives and friends giving her their pity and the ridiculous phrase 'Things will get better in time' when they knew nothing of the inner turmoil inevitably tearing her insides to shreds. I'd helped her escape her pain for a short while.

"Thank you. Would...would it be ok to call you sometime? Unless you don't..."

"No, I don't mind," I interrupted, surprised to find I meant it. She stared at me, as if she hadn't expected me to say yes, but then she nodded gently. Without another word, she turned and exited the room, shutting the door softly behind her. I fell back on the bed and covered my face with the pillow, which is how I stayed for the next hour until I dragged myself up and out of the motel.

It was already ridiculously hot outside and the ride home was refreshingly cool, if not longer than it should have been, but I didn't want to push things in my delicate state. I hoped mom wasn't in a quizzical mood – I just wanted to relax and try to put things out of my mind for a while. When I parked up, I could see mom in the window and I waved curiously before going inside.

"You know that big ole house 'cross the road? There's been removal trucks parked outside all morning. Not just one, but three!" Mom was stood unashamedly peering out of our front window and I could tell from her excited tone she'd been there for a while waiting for someone to talk to about this turn of events. The house across the road had been empty for nearly two years after the previous occupant had killed his brother and father before turning the shotgun on himself. To this day, no one knew what had caused the tragedy, although there'd been a lot of speculation that the boys had been suffering abuse at the hands of their father since their mom died when they were very young. (Died in *suspicious circumstances*, as everyone round here was very quick to point out.)

I rolled my eyes and went to the kitchen to make some coffee and breakfast but stopped in the doorway. Or rather, the vile aroma surrounding the kitchen like a nuclear cloud stopped me. I recoiled, wrinkling my nose in an effort to reject the smell as my hangover threatened to empty my stomach.

"Er, mom, what happened in the kitchen?"

Sheepishly, mom cast a quick glance in the general direction, as if even looking at it was too much for her eyes to bear.

"Oh that? That was your dinner honey."

"Mm. I had no idea you hated me that much?" I mumbled, frowning. "What was it? Y'know, just so I can make sure I don't come home next time you cook it for me?"

"It was a beef stew but I thought I'd experiment a little. Who woulda thought brandy doesn't mix well with beef?"

"You...you put brandy in the beef stew?" I asked incredulously. "And what other crazy capers did ya get up to while you were possessed last night? A little naked dancing on the front porch?"

"Quickly! A car's just pulled up! I just bet it's the new owner," Mom near enough screeched, beckoning me wildly with one arm. Despite myself, I hurried across the room to see who was going to step out of the car, and had a strange image in my head of all our neighbours doing the same thing. This part of Siloam Springs was very much like that — everyone wanted to know everyone else's business without having to actually ask them about it. According to mom, gossiping and spying through curtains was the best way to get accurate information because, let's face it — no one was going to voluntarily tell you anything if it was juicy or sensitive. When I'd argued that maybe those sort of things were meant to be private, she'd raised her eyebrows and said, "Nothing's private round here, sweetheart. Remember the time your father tried to have you committed - everybody and their mother came out to watch the ambulance take you away." Even though it reinforced my argument, she looked like she'd delivered the winning shot to the discussion we'd been having. I let her have it, but only because it wasn't worth taking it further.

We both watched eagerly as the car doors opened and four people emerged. The elder two, parents I assumed, stretched their limbs while looking up at their new home. The younger kids from the back, a cute guy in his early twenties and a girl of about seven years old decided to study the street instead, seeming curious but pleased with what they saw. But it was the mom that caught my eye as she jogged excitedly up to the front door, beckoning the others enthusiastically. She had dark hair that fell just short of her shoulders and was wearing a skimpy vest and shorts. *Short* shorts.

"Maybe I should make them a cake?" Mom said beside me in a hushed whisper.

"What, you want them to move out already?" I winced as my rib was poked.

"Don't be cheeky young lady. Wait, what's this? Oh my sweet Lord!"

I followed her gaze — a minibus had pulled up behind the car and about nine others, all of various ages and races, were piling out onto the street. The kids from the car greeted them before they all headed up to the house en masse.

"Oh my sweet Lord!" Mom repeated slowly, her eyes wide. "It's one of those religious cults!"

I spluttered a laugh.

"Maybe you're right? Maybe I should go over and welcome them to the neighbourhood?" I suggested.

"No! Absolutely not! I don't want you going anywhere near that house Nikki!"

"What? But why? I can get all the inside info for you before anyone else!"

"Now you just listen to me. I'm not losing the only daughter I have, and ever will have, to some kooky cult that goes around brainwashing influential youngsters, d'you hear me?" Mom hissed vehemently.

"But..."

"No!"

"Aw mom..."

"No, Nikki! And that's final."

*** *** ***

Two hours later, I walked nervously up to the front door and gave a gentle rap. I could feel mom's eyes burning into the back of my neck and predicted she was gently murmuring to herself 'Don't drink or eat anything they offer you — just go in, be polite, find out why they're here and get out of there!' I smirked to myself as I imagined it, but then the door opened and a young hispanic girl of about sixteen leaned against the door.

"Oh. Hey."

"Hi."

I suddenly couldn't think of what to say. I didn't want to ask if her mom was home, because unless she'd been very busy with a lot of men over the years, they clearly weren't all her kids. So I just stared at her for a few awkward seconds before finding my tongue.

"Uh...I'm from across the road over there, and I thought I'd come over and introduce myself, welcome you in 'n' all." I shuffled my feet as she stared back, not knowing whether or not I should just go. But then the hot shorts lady suddenly appeared.

"Who's at the door, Lisa? Oh, hello," she greeted warmly, smiling as she extended her hand to me. I shook it and smiled back, repeating what I'd just said to Lisa. Her smile grew. "Wow, gee that's so nice of you! Please come in. Can I get you a drink?"

"Sure, that'd be great. My name's Nikki."

"I'm Amanda. I hope Kool Aid is ok? We haven't really gotten round to unpacking all the kitchen boxes yet."

I couldn't help smiling — mom would have a baby if she knew I was accepting Kool Aid! As I followed Amanda through to the kitchen, I was surprised at how quiet it was, having expected more noise from the horde in the minibus. Also, a lot of the unpacking had already been tackled and I put that down to the volume of people working hard to get the house liveable in.

"Would you like some cake? It was made for the journey, but we have quite a lot leftover."

"I love cake," I replied, smiling wider. I watched her closely as she hunted out a large cool box and fished inside for the cake and drink, admiring her body which was bathed in a light sheen of sweat from unpacking. Up close I'd put her at mid to late forties, and even more beautiful than I'd originally thought. She had hazel eyes and I was instantly attracted. A small voice inside tutted in disgust at how quickly poor Poppy had been forgotten and left behind, but I ignored it. She held out a hunk of what looked like apple cake on a bed of foil and a plastic beaker of Kool Aid.

"Here you go. So, did you really come over to welcome us in, or are you here to find out who we are and why there's so many of us?"

My hand froze halfway to my mouth with the cake. She was looking at me with an amused but knowing expression on her face, and I chuckled.

"Busted! Although, it was a bit of both to be honest" I admitted, deciding to come clean with her. She nodded and tucked some hair behind her ear.

"Can't say I blame you. We must seem like a bit of an odd bunch, huh?"

"I think it's fair to say your arrival didn't go unnoticed." I took a mouthful of the cake, which was delicious and moist with sultanas and cinnamon and a hint of nutmeg. "This is really good!" I said, hoping she wouldn't think me rude talking with a semi-full mouth of cake, but she just laughed.

"Thank you. Our neighbours made it for us before we left so I can't accept the credit sadly." She leaned casually against the sink, thinking. I waited patiently, devouring what could only be described as the best apple cake I'd ever tasted. "Mike and I started this little group about seven years ago, and we seem to have grown more than we ever anticipated. Would you like the full story or are you in a rush?"

"If I go home with anything less than the full story, my mom will only send me back" I said and Amanda laughed again.

"Well, I hope you're open minded? Ok, let me see...I think it all began when a boy in our street, Corey, started getting bullied because he was gay. He was only fifteen but he'd made the mistake of confiding in one of his so called friends and his life got turned upside down. His parents didn't wanna know and offered him no support, his older brother practically spearheaded the bullying against him and he had no one to turn to. So he tried to take his own life, not just once but three times, which is when his parents had him committed at the hospital. But when he came out, everything just continued as it had before he'd gone in.

So one day, I'm in the kitchen doing dinner for Mike and Nessa, our daughter, and Mike comes rushing out telling me to get a bowl of hot water and the med kit. He'd seen Corey being beaten on out in the street and chased them off with a bat, then brought Corey inside. He was in a pretty bad way – I wanted to take him to the hospital, but he got agitated at the mere mention of it, so we just tended his wounds as best we could with what we had. To cut a long story short, Corey started to come over every day at our insistence. Our place became a sanctuary for him after school, and then he'd go home to sleep in the evenings until eventually we offered him our spare room. His family didn't notice or didn't care so we kinda became his surrogate family, and that was roundabout the time Mike told me he was bi-sexual."

I actually spat a mouthful of grape Kool Aid down my chin in surprise at her openly admitting this so soon after my walking through the door. She laughed at my reaction.

"We don't believe in hiding who we are, Nikki. And you did say you wanted the full story."

"Absolutely do. Please carry on," I said, trying to regain my cool composure.

"Speak of the devil. Mike, this is Nikki from across the street. She's come to welcome us."

Her husband entered the kitchen and immediately came to warmly shake my hand as we said our hellos.

"Amanda was just telling me the background on, er, you guys" I said, flushing red. I wasn't sure how he was going to react to his wife being so forthcoming with the family history.

"In that case, I'll leave you both to it. We've nearly unpacked all the bedroom furniture so everyone's got a bed to sleep in tonight," he said, looking through some of the boxes. "Aha! Here it is. Sara-Lynn remembered putting it in one of the kitchen boxes for some strange reason." He held up a small see through bag with knobs and screws in it.

"Good job, honey. I'll get back to unpacking the kitchen soon."

"Don't worry about it, I'll send some of the others down. You keep our guest entertained. Nice to meet you Nikki, don't be a stranger." They kissed lightly before he walked quickly out.

"You good for me to carry on?" Amanda asked and I nodded.

Over the next half hour, she told me how they'd had set up their home as a refuge for anyone suffering at the hands of racists, bullies, homophobes and practiced what they liked to call 'Free Love.' When I asked what Free Love was, she said simply, 'Being free to love whoever you want, whenever you want.'

It was fair to say I was very excited!

I finally ventured home with the promise of returning again very soon, and so many thoughts racing round my head. I was totally sold on their Free Love house and if it was a cult, I was definitely ready to sign up!

Mom was gonna have kittens!

"They do what?"

I stifled a smile. Or rather tried to. The huge grin spreading across my face was hard to hide, and I had to wonder if maybe they had put something in the Kool Aid? Or maybe that cake? Damn, it *had* been good.

"They open their home to anyone who needs it. Like gay kids who have been disowned by their families and stuff. It's a prejudice free house."

This was, of course, the easy-to-digest-for-my-mom version. If I told her they promoted Free Love, it would be all over the neighbourhood that they were a whore house promoting free sex quicker than not.

"Oh my sweet Lord!" This was fast turning into her mantra for today. "But there's so many of them. Did you find out where they're all sleeping? What if it's a house of sin? Right across from us!" She lowered her tone and volume. "It's the house! It's cursed!"

I laughed out loud, knowing this was going to turn into her new obsession for a very long time. Such a juicy story would keep her occupied for weeks, months even.

"Ok mom, well I'm going out back to my studio to do some work. Don't keep me any dinner. Please." I added, winking at her. But she was already distracted back to twitching at the window when the phone rang.

"Hello? She just got back. Apparently, it's a free house..."

I left her telling whichever one of our neighbours it was on the phone a distorted version of what I'd told her and went to my work studio in the backyard.

The second I closed the door, I felt a degree of serenity settle over me in contrast to the craziness of the last week. This was my place, my haven, my sanctuary. I'd had this studio for the better part of my teenage years and created my first works of art here. I smiled as I remembered my first sell — it had been for fifty dollars and I'd been so pumped, I'd gone out and blown a hundred dollars celebrating it. That had been seven years ago and now that piece was probably valued at least a few hundred times its original cost, possibly more. My paintings sold for an average of three to five thousand dollars these days, and even though I was pretty well established in the art world now, it was hard not to feel the pressure of producing a masterpiece each time.

I was currently in the middle of a commission from some big city hotshot and couldn't wait to get it finished so I could return to free-styling. He'd been pretty specific about what he wanted, and even though it was do-able, it was hard going for me. But the money was definitely worth the struggle.

*** *** ***

By the time I emerged from my studio, it was dark and almost time for me to go to bed. I'd made some good progress on the piece, as I always did when I had stuff playing on my mind. I don't know why it was, but it just was. That wasn't to say I wanted, nor welcomed drama in my life, but hey. What was the alternative? Living in poverty like Nick, wondering where my next meal was coming from? (Although if she quit smoking, she might be able to eat more, but that was never going to happen.)

Mom had already hit the sack, so I crept quietly up so as not to disturb her. She no doubt had a busy day planned tomorrow watching our new neighbours (as I also planned, but one in particular!)

I was starting to feel my eyes droop as I brushed my teeth and hurried — not because I was in a hurry to wake up as her, as Nick, but because I had no control over the 'falling asleep' and didn't want to pass out on the bathroom floor. Again.

In bed, I barely managed to get comfortable before I felt myself drifting off. When I next opened my eyes, I would be Nick...and I'd have to deal with a whole lot of Scottish shit.

CHAPTER FOUR

How did I get to this day? A question I am constantly reciting with every new consciousness. Where has that sun come from, the one who invades my room, shoving himself in my windows and heating my floor? Dare I open my eyes tomorrow and hope that the warmth you bring will not be to my wood but to my life?

Quiet now. Listen. What is that noise?

It's the beat of my heart, never missing a trick, keeping me going, ready to warm me in the glare of the sun's rays. I am ageing, that warming love laying the lines that will grow on my skin, furrows I will never fill. Only Helena can touch me and take away the pain. Where has she been? Why did she go? Will she be back tomorrow?

Will she be back tomorrow? Will I get to then?

I opened my eyes, blinking at the horror of daylight and grabbed my phone. There were no missed calls. For ten years, I have had the same number, a number that Helena knows but that she has never called. Not since she disappeared. And she could have. What does it take to punch in a text to say, "I am okay?" It takes nothing.

Ingenting. Nothing is all I have.

"Mum?" I say into my phone.

"Nick? Are you okay, honey?"

I swallow my pride. "I need some money." I hear the silence. The seconds tick on.

"How much this time?" she says finally.

"Five hundred."

"Okay."

"It's not for me," I tell her, the guilt ripping through me. "It's for Mr Chan, the Private Dick I hired to find Helena."

"Oh, Nick," she sighed. "Why?"

"He's found her."

"Do you ever think she doesn't want to be found?"

"Will you send the money or not?"

"Honey, yes, of course I will. I just want you to be happy."

"This makes me happy."

"What about that dinner with Freya?"

I thought back to the soft folds of Freya's arms around me, pulling me into her, feeling the insistence of her breasts into me, her nipples hardening against me.

"It was fine." I hung up.

I cannot be in the middle of two women. One burning heart is enough to flip my life into a turmoil I cannot recover from. Love has woven around me, like a spider's thick web, keeping me away from anyone else because harsh, silken woes protect me. Shiny webs of fear that I use to deceive myself, and if I try to step away, they anchor me to the same spot in life. I need some ice to kill the fire that burns away inside.

When my door knocked, I jumped, because no-one ever visited me. I have made sure my anti-social attitude and unwavering cynicism keep at bay unwanted attention and yet...

And yet... I long for arms to hold me and never let go.

I opened the door to the friendly smile of Freya and stood aside to let her in.

"I wanted to talk about our last night," she began, swirling into the room with her bare feet gliding across my wooden floor. I could see the path she had danced and found myself following her footsteps, as though a spell had been placed. She pirouetted to face me, her dress floating above her knees, teasing me with a hint of thigh.

"I'm sorry," I started. Making apologies was nothing new to me.

"Nei, nei," she said and for a second her blue eyes sparkled, two sapphires lost in a blanket of snow. It stopped me in my tracks because I am not often taken aback by beauty and I was then, in that tiny moment.

Nothing frightens me more than love.

"I know you are delicate in your soul," Freya said. "I push on you too much."

I tried to think back through the muddle of memories and dark spots to Freya's soft lips on mine. I felt a jerk inside at the erotic sensation of our brief dalliance remembering itself in me.

I shook my head. "It was me. I thought I could… and I couldn't. I'm sorry." It was an apology that was genuine.

"You *can*," she said, walking towards me, laying her right cheek on my chest, just above my left breast where my heart was beating fiercely. Her back ached for my arms to go around but they lay lifeless by my side. "Let me in to your heart. I feel it."

In my head, I swallowed a mouthful of fear and tried not to cry. Terror was taking over me and I tried to find the strength to fight the dazzling purity of Freya and the horrifying absence of Helena. I didn't know which was worse.

"I feel your heart," she repeated.

I swallowed hard again, trying to find words that would not betray me because the last thing I wanted to do was reveal what I am.

Before I could speak, my mother had let herself in, carrying bags of shopping. Freya, hearing the door creak open, wrenched herself upright but she still glowed.

"Nick, sweetheart, I've been to 'Tesco'. I can't bear to think of you starving away…" She stopped mid-sentence, her face immediately lighting up seeing I had company. "You must be Freya. I'm Nick's mum."

Freya smiled from one end of my room to the other, engulfing us in her happiness. "I am Freya, I live underneath. I am very pleased to meet you, *Mor*."

I rolled my eyes. "Freya, just call her Ethel. I do."

My mum had already walked over to my open plan kitchen, dumped the bags and had begun to unpack and put away the groceries. "It's lovely to meet you, Freya. I've heard a lot of nice things about you."

Freya's eyebrows hit the ceiling in joy and she clasped her hands together in front of her chest. "Oh no, Nick tells lies, don't believe what she says," she laughed.

This was somewhere on the list of my worst nightmares but knowing my mother as I did, I knew there was no way out. In any case, I needed her cash. I would need to get rid of Freya because I didn't want her knowing what I was doing.

Why was I held back from telling her what I was up to if I only loved Helena? I am still a person and I still need a passion. I have fires that need flames.

I saw a ray of sunshine glide its way across my floor and I looked through it, to my mum, hands on her hips, having filled my fridge.

"Nick, here is the money you asked for." She threw down a fat envelope onto a work surface.

"Thank you," I mumbled.

"Did she tell you, Freya, about this obsession she has with an old flame?" I could have choked Ethel!

"Nei," Freya said, glancing at me.

I blew out air. I could have been a successful artist, living in America with women falling at my feet. Or I could be battering my body off the padded walls of an enclosed cell. What is the difference?

I wanted to reach out my hands — to Nikki — and take over the life I was meant to lead, to have fame and money at my fingertips, where love would welcome me and build me a home. I could rest my head without panic.

The grass is always greener on the other side.

"She's got a private detective chasing an old girlfriend that she hasn't seen for years," Ethel went on.

I looked to Freya and saw her unwavering smile falter. I realised then that inside of her, she too hid a broken heart. I could have moved towards her then, but my feet were cemented to where I stood. Fear is the heaviest weight of all.

Freya.

Helena.

Love. Fear. Death. The perfect circle of life.

"…Five hundred pounds, Freya, for nothing. Can you talk some sense into her?"

I came back to the sadness of this life I was leading and found my antagonistic tongue. "Thanks for the money. Thanks for the food. There's the door."

Ethel, my mum, wagged her finger at me. "I don't agree with this, Nick. It will all end in tears."

"Jesus," I sighed. I noticed that the sun was shining through the material of the dress Freya was wearing, a loose sky-blue temptation. I almost felt my fingers run up her thighs, over her hips to her tummy until they could cup her…I wanted to throw her roughly to my floor, put myself between her legs to rip off her pants and push my face into her. I licked my lips at the tickle of her on my chin and felt her wet my lips as I opened her with my tongue, my hands grabbing her buttocks, pushing her into me. I'd lick her, my rhythm growing until she flexed her hips again and again, her moans filling my ears and, as she was about to come, my fingers would slide inside her, feeling the tensing and her ecstasy…

"Nick!"

I saw Freya, standing before me, innocent and ready to be loved. I closed my eyes and saw Helena. Helena tossing her hair over her shoulder, Helena running her eyes over me, Helena reaching out to kiss me, Helena saying, "Don't ever give up on me."

I won't ever give up, my Helena.

"NICK!"

"Mum! What?"

"Do you ever listen?" she said, looking sympathetically towards Freya. "Let me know what Mr Chan says."

I nodded and she left. I still had a throb in my underwear that made me unable to speak.

"I want you to paint me," Freya said, wandering towards my canvas, covered and hidden.

"I'll only paint you nude," I told her.

"I'm not ashamed of my body," she said. "I'm Norwegian, not English."

"I'm not English, either," I clipped back. "I'm Scottish."

She smiled, then turned and walked to my wall of windows, throwing her dress to the floor and stepping out as she made her way over.

"Mum," I wanted to say, "There's a naked Norwegian in my living-room." An ice-hot, sexy, naked Norwegian who is filling my mind with clouds, my heart with doubts and my body with desires. It won't do but I don't know how to fight. You can't defeat love with love.

"Are you going to start now, Nick?" Freya asked.

I smiled, fizzing inside at the crisp curves of her hips and thighs, of her breasts and the shadow on her navel. "I am. Turn a fraction to my right."

She turned. "How fine is this?"

"It's gallus," I said.

"Ha, I don't know that word, Nikki," she laughed.

I felt the vein bulge at my temple. "Don't call me Nikki!"

It took me to a time in my past, a memory surfaced that I had tried to bury, like so many other things.

19

Helena and I were alone in her parents home, the music was loud and we had drunk our fair share of the wine cellar. I never felt happier than when I had her to myself, when I could hold her body close to mine, sweating with her heat. I was swaying to Roxy Music's 'Slave to Love', pulling her so close I could feel her breath on my lips and my excitement was growing. I swayed left and right, my hips finding their best sexy rhythm against her as I stared into her brown eyes, dark and full of promise.

Or so I had thought then.

I whispered into her ear, trying to be seductive. "Let's take this to your bedroom."

She panted because she was aching for what I would do to her, knowing full well the extent of my devotion and my dedication to her pleasure. The only thing I desired was her ecstasy and feeling it under my fingertips. It was the only thing in my miserable life that gave me a glimpse of happiness.

It was a childhood I spent hating school and hating people, I hated everything but Helena. I hid under the blanket of her protection but my... *my oddness*... kept me separate. I could not allow myself to get close to anyone, not when one day was never where the next ought to be and my life switched before me like changing sands.

Helena was my only constant.

Whenever I woke up, she was in my mind and sometimes, I could lay the palm of my hand on her brow and imagine the mechanics of her mind. I'd try to let them seep into mine, to keep me normal, to keep me tethered to this life, a second in a life where I felt loved. Where I had a life that was mine and no-one else's. Where falling asleep and closing my eyes didn't mean succumbing to another self, where daydreams might actually be real if I had the courage it would take for that.

What would it take? I couldn't answer that.

Just then, Helena plunged her tongue into my mouth and I responded, feeding her pants with my fingers, playing braille in the way I knew she loved to be read.

"Oh, baby," she breathed into my neck.

I thrust myself in, loving her pleasure.

"Oh, baby. Oh, Nikki."

I froze.

I am not Nikki.

I am *not* fucking Nikki.

I whipped my hand from Helena's pants, still glistening with her passion, and I slid my fingers around her neck, pressing her against the wall, feeling the muscles in her neck arch against my pressure.

"I'm not fucking Nikki!" I told her.

"You're hurting me," she choked.

I pushed her harder against the wall, seeing her face turn redder as her hands tugged at mine. How could she call me Nikki? Didn't she know me? I could never be Nikki.

I have my secret and Nikki has hers and we are as different as night and day. Night brings dark, black, quiet and the fear that the day before was a waste. I live in the night and all my days before are a waste.

I don't and never want to be Nikki. I pressed my fingers tighter around Helena's throat, feeling betrayed by her throwaway comment.

I am Nick! Me. *Nick*. I have a heart so soft I want to take buttercups and stare at the yellow glow they make under Helena's chin. I would take that buttercup and trample it underfoot because it reminded me of the love gone wrong.

It's not me, it's not me, it's not fucking me.

I AM ME!

I push my hands harder, gritting my teeth, saying "I'm me, not fucking Nikki. Helena, I'm Nick."

*** *** ***

It took a moment for the fear and the pain to fade away into distant memory but it left me with horror running up my arms to tickle my neck. I could have killed Helena for a slip of the tongue and where would that have left me and my love? Can a heart beat on when it has nothing left to love?

What fills an empty heart? Love. There is nothing else.

I looked at Freya and my hand found its way to the canvas, as it always does. My eyes and my hand connected and I lost myself in the colours and contours, in the shadows and the brightness. In the beauty that stood before me.

In the midnight blue of beauty.

I once saw the moon shine in a window, into eyes which were of the ocean and the glare made them midnight blue. In the blue of midnight stands me, Nick. I used to be a woman who had colour in everything I did and now I am just midnight blue.

But midnight blue is still better than black.

So, I took my brush and I let it light up my canvas with the sparkle that was Freya's delight. It took me moments in my head to see the beauty and to do it justice. I tried and I squinted and I saw her gorgeous appeal but what I felt was not curves and shadows of light, it was a softness in her eyes and the ache I could feel inside of her, the one that reached out to me.

My mind touched hers.

I moved to Freya and I put my hand on her throat.

"People think you are so angry," she said. "But you are just sad."

My hand slid up her neck to her cheek.

"There's a truth inside of you that you can't bear to face. But you'll have to face it one day. Don't *vaere trist*."

I could help myself no longer and I jutted my chin until her lips were touching mine, and I whispered, "I've seen love. I've followed before and I'll follow again."

Her mouth opened and we found a rhythm inside each other and my simple heart broke in two.

There was a moment when Helena held me and I did nothing to resist and then that moment came when Freya put her stamp on me and that was what it took for me to lose myself. I heard the shuffle on my music centre bring up the next song, 'Slave to Love' and I shuddered with the fear in my heart.

I am so scared to be wrong. I am so scared to love someone who does not deserve me but I am more scared to love someone who does. Because what if I love Freya and let her in to my heart and she overtakes me, fuelling every flame inside me? Then I die.

I don't care, I don't care. I would rather be dead than live without love.

I threw my brush to the floor and I took her naked body in my arms, overwhelmed by desire. It's been years since I looked at a woman with a passion that wasn't faked. I've thrown a veil around my heart to keep me from feeling and Freya had pulled it off, opening me up to longing.

I long to feel once more. It has taken a glacier to thaw me and bring me heat. I lay naked beside Freya on my floor, a few hours later, having covered us with the quilt off my bed. She lay smiling quietly at me and I smiled back, a real smile, not one of my forced grimaces. It's been a long time since I've known contentedness.

"You are beautiful," I whispered. I meant her soul.

"*Vakker*," she said.

21

"Vakker," I agreed, not knowing what her word meant but liking how it rolled off her tongue which made me kiss her again.

"Oh, your *lidenskap* finds me," she sighed.

But I had more to find than Freya's passion and finally, I forced us up to get dressed, throwing a sheet over my unfinished painting.

"You'll have to come back," I said. "I've only just begun."

She twirled in her dress. "I will always be back."

I walked to my kitchen area to make a cup of tea and saw the envelope of cash that Ethel had left. I inhaled, remembering why it was there, turning it over in my hands.

I jumped, at the surprise of Freya's arms snaking round me, to hold me tight around my tummy. I wasn't used to being held and the wave of emotion this brought on rose from my stomach to form a lump in my throat. I swallowed down that feeling, cleared my throat and said, "I have to go out."

"I am going to be with you," Freya said.

"I know that," I answered, maybe too harshly.

"I mean I am going to be with you when you go looking for old lovers."

She made me sound desperate. I mean, I was but I didn't need Scandinavian reminders. I shook her arms off. "You're not coming."

She turned me and met my eyes with hers and beyond the ice was steel. "I will be beside you now," she said, stamping her right foot.

An hour later, we sat waiting for Mr Chan to call me into his office. He employed a faded blonde, whose youthful looks were well behind her, to man his reception in an effort to appear respectable but, below this veneer, he was just a 'hunt the cunt' like so many others.

"What are you going to get from here?" Freya asked, while we sat leafing through magazines without looking at the pages.

"I'm going to get Helena's new address and then I'm going to visit her. There are words inside me that need to find their way to her ears before I can rest a single second."

"*Drommer*," she scoffed.

I shuffled in my chair, knowing she was being uncomplimentary but before I could retort, Mr Chan's door opened and his sleazy smile welcomed us in.

I felt the old armour grow around me as I walked forward into battle. I never thought love would be a battle and I was right; it's not a battle, it's a war that never ends. As I walked in, I felt Freya's hand clasp hold of mine and I was heart-warmed by the thought she wanted to stand strong beside me.

It's easy to be strong when you don't know what you are standing against or who you are standing with.

"So, you have money?" Mr Chan said, sitting back down behind his desk, rubbing his hands over his oily hair.

I threw the envelope of cash in front of him, which he opened and counted meticulously. Satisfied, he unlocked a drawer, stashed the money and locked it back up. "So, you want address, yes?"

"Aye," I managed through gritted teeth. I could not pretend to like the man but he had done his job and that demanded my manners. Ethel would have been so proud of me.

"I find," he said, getting up and heading to a filing cabinet in the corner of the room.

Freya had not let go of my hand.

The seconds ticked on and my hand grew warm. In the dark office, a single ray shone in, highlighting the dust fixed in the air, specks of animation that were frozen for a milli-second in time.

"Here," he said, giving me an A4 page with three small typed lines. I withdrew my hand from Freya's and folded it, standing up to tuck it into the back pocket of my jeans.

"Come on," I said to Freya, heading for the door.

"No thank you?" Mr Chan wailed after me.

"Cheers, Jackie," I said, holding open the door for Freya.

He lowered his brows. "Name no Jackie!"

"Fuck you," I laughed, slamming his door shut behind me.

I had Helena's address resting against my right buttock. I had Freya's breasts a fingertip away. If I closed my eyes and squinted I might be able, by a long stretch, to see a gateway to happiness.

CHAPTER FIVE

I spent most of the morning in my studio trying to think of a valid excuse to go back over to the new neighbours, and unable to think of one that didn't sound too flimsy. I assumed mom was spending just as much time watching them, because she now appeared to be camping out by the window.

As I idly studied my work in progress on the canvas before me, I wondered if Amanda practiced her free love with women. I wondered if Amanda would be interested in showing me a little bit of free love. I wondered if she was the kind of woman who let her pubic hair grow wild and free, or if she waxed? From my own deductions based on what I knew of her, I was willing to bet she let it grow free, but kept it tidy. Now all I had to do was figure out a way to validate my theory.

Just before noon, I decided I wasn't going to get anything productive done and headed inside for an update from mom, and some lunch.

"Any activity to report, soldier?" I hissed, after creeping up on her position, but she didn't even flinch.

"Papa bear left this morning with three of the youngsters, another two went for a jog an hour ago and haven't returned yet, and Momma bear hasn't emerged yet," she muttered conspiratorially.

"Momma and Papa bear? Seriously?"

She ignored me and picked up a blanket she was making (with the same amount of enthusiasm as I'd put into my canvas this morning. It worried me that I could see where I got it from so clearly.)

I decided to leave her to it and went to fix myself a grilled cheese sandwich for my lunch, noting how empty the refrigerator was at the same time. When was the last time either of us had gone out for groceries? Sighing as I waited for the pan to warm up, I knew I wouldn't be getting any more work done today as I took care of the necessities around the house. It was kind of ironic in a way — here, I took care of mom, gave her money to get by and looked after the bills and stuff, whereas Nick sponged off her mother and expected to have everything done for her. Perhaps if she got off her butt and did something with her life she might be able to cope with life as well as deal with her anger issues. She just made me so frustrated.

I was shaken from my thoughts by mom hurtling out to the kitchen, a frantic look on her face.

"Over here! She's coming over here!" she squealed, waving her hands and reminding me of Wallace from 'Wallace and Gromit' with her exaggerated mannerisms and wide eyes. I stifled a laugh.

"Who?" My heart skipped as the information sank in and I became deadly serious. "Not Momma bear?"

"Yes! What did you..."

Mom was interrupted by a polite knocking on the front door. Her jaw dropped open in wonderful comic style. We both stared at the door for a few seconds, unsure who should go answer it. After a quick visual sweep of myself, I trotted excitedly to the door, closely followed by mom gripping my elbow. I shook her free before taking a deep breath, adopting a casual stance and opening the door.

"Oh, hi Amanda, how nice to see you."

"Hey Nikki, I hope you don't mind my coming over like this, but I need to go into town and I have no idea where I'm going." She laughed easily and my heart laughed with her. "Ness needs me to pick her up from the ice rink and I didn't want to leave her standing waiting for me, so I just wondered if you were free for part of that sightseeing tour you promised?"

Oh happy, happy, joy joy!

"Uh, yeah of course..."

"If you're busy..."

"Nope, I'm all yours! Let me just get my stuff and I'll meet you at your car in a couple of minutes," I gushed, trying not to sound too eager or desperate. Inside I felt like an excitable puppy straining against the leash, tongue hanging wildly out to one side as I panted hopelessly for her. As long as I restrained myself from trying to hump her leg, I should be A-O-K!

"Great. And thank you."

I watched her walk all the way back across to her car before I remembered mom, and as I shut the door, she was just about ready to burst.

"Nikki, what did I tell you about staying clear of them?"

"Mom, come on. They're actually really nice. Anyway, I thought you'd be happy having someone on the inside?" I said, rushing to find my keys and shades.

"It's making sure you get back out safe that's worrying me."

"I'll be fine! They're just normal people," I insisted, giving her a quick peck on the cheek. "There's a grilled cheese sandwich in the kitchen you can have for your lunch, and I'll get some shopping later, okay? Bye."

I ran out of the door and practically skipped to Amanda's car, unable to stop from grinning stupidly at her as I got in.

"Hope you don't mind Mika?" She said with a sheepish smile.

"What?" I looked into the back, wondering if she had a pet I didn't know about.

"Mika the singer? Kev put one of his cd's in the cd player a couple of months ago and then the whole machine kinda frazzled. None of the buttons work anymore so it plays on constant repeat at the same volume." She turned to me and shook her head gently. "No-one's forgiven him for it yet I don't think."

"Well, I've never heard of Mika, so I should be okay for a few rounds either way." I would have listened to anything on repeat if it meant sitting next to this beautiful woman. Today she was wearing lemon shorts and a white vest that showed off the muscles in her arms and I had to look away before I leaned forward and licked them or something stupid.

"So, which way to the rink?"

I gave her a few brief directions, smiling as we pulled away and an enthusiastic voice from the stereo encouraged that 'Everybody's gotta love today, love today, love today, any way you want to, any way you got to, love love me.'

It was only a fifteen minute drive and she seemed surprised when we pulled into the almost empty car park so soon. As Ness wasn't due to finish for another forty-five minutes she offered to buy me lunch while we waited, and after ordering a couple of burgers, we took seats near the rink.

"I didn't know it was open this early," I admitted, before sinking my teeth into the greasy mess that barely passed as edible.

"It's not open to the public, no. But Ness is a figure skater, so most rinks make certain exceptions for things like that, especially if it can bring publicity their way."

I raised my eyebrows. She'd introduced me to Ness when I'd gone round the other day and she'd come across as extremely shy and geeky. I'd have put her down as a science enthusiast rather than a figure skater? It was something I had trouble picturing, until Amanda turned her head and pointed, talking politely through a mouthful of burger.

"There she is, in the green dress."

I stared confused at the sexy, confident woman currently breezing around the ice like she owned it, then stopped chewing altogether when she did a few leaps and spins (which I couldn't remember the technical terms for.) As she moved with the music that I was only just now hearing, i realised it was one of my favourites – Beethoven's *Moonlight Sonata*. Already a haunting tune, she captured the essence of it in every way, from the soulful way she was gliding to the mournful expressions on her face. My body erupted in goosebumps as I swallowed a lump of barely masticated food.

"She's very good," I murmured, not taking my eyes off her for a second. Amanda laughed.

"You could say that. She's also very pissed with me. A couple of months ago a scout saw her winning a local competition and asked her to come and try out for Nationals, but she didn't want to. I told him to send the forms anyway and when the application arrived I kinda intercepted it and filled it in for her. They're sending another scout down to watch her pretty soon, so she's nervous as a cat in a room full of rocking chairs under all the pressure."

She certainly didn't look nervous. She just looked ethereal, sublime, beautiful. She fed my eyes and my soul with her expression of the music and...

"Hello? Nikki?"

I turned my head, unaware Amanda had been talking to me. She was looking at me curiously, almost amused, as if fully aware of my train of thought. Blushing, I gave her a questioning look, hoping she'd repeat the question.

"I asked you what sort of paintings you create."

"Oh. Yes." I knew that wasn't an answer, but for the life of me I couldn't think! Every fibre in my being was trying to turn my attention back to the ice, like a pair of invisible giant hands, but I needed to act cool so I frowned in an effort to concentrate, and stared up at the ceiling instead. "All sorts really, but mostly abstract. I like deep, dark colours." There! Cool on every level.

"Would I be able to come and see some of your work?"

"Sure. I've only got a few pieces in my studio, but they're personal and not for sale. Everything else goes to galleries, or is commissioned."

"And how much do you charge for a commission?"

"I guess it depends on how much work is involved, whether it's something I'll enjoy or find tedious, but mainly how much they can afford to pay."

"You'd charge less for someone who couldn't afford you and give them the same quality as someone who said money was no limit?" Amanda asked, looking surprised.

"Sure. I'm not so egotistical that I think only the rich should be able to have one of my pieces. I paint because I enjoy it, and I want other people to enjoy what I do as well. I don't need the money." I don't know why I felt the urge to justify myself to her, but it was an argument I'd had so many times with mom that the words fell easily out of my mouth.

"Hey, I wasn't knocking you. I was just thinking it's a shame there aren't more like you in the world. You're right, art should be enjoyed by everyone."

Amanda shifted her attention to Ness so I took the opportunity to copy suit as we concentrated on her and our food for a while.

"So, are you dating anyone at the moment, Nikki?"

"What? Uh, no." Her sudden question made me feel uneasy and I put the remnants of the greasy burger on the table in front of me. Evidently being head of a house of mixed ages meant you gained a skill of super-perceptibility because I felt her watching me carefully.

"Just break up with someone?" she asked gently. I knew if I told her I didn't want to talk about it, she'd respect my wishes. But I *did* want to talk about it.

"It's kinda complicated. And a little depressing. You probably don't want me to bore you with it," I muttered. She put her hand on my arm.

"Try me."

I sighed, trying to put into words what had been eating me up for the last fortnight.

"Well, I guess it all started four weeks ago. I was out in the fields watching the clouds, y'know, for inspiration? It helps clear my mind sometimes. So anyway, I was feeling all relaxed and I heard a horse coming."

I smiled softly, remembering.

It wasn't just a horse approaching. It was a horse with a beautiful vision riding it, long, dark, wild hair fanning behind her as she leaned forward. Her face was flushed and excited, as if she'd done something mischievous and was making a quick getaway. She caught sight of me and made a detour my way. I mentally prepared myself to act cool, but I had a huge thing for cowgirls. *Huge.*

She jumped off when she reached me.

"Hey! Wow, it feels good to be riding today," she enthused, taking a canteen of water and swigging from it before offering it to me.

"I guess. I haven't ridden in years. I got a motorcycle and it kinda took over my life," I admitted, trying not to stare at her eyes. Up close, she resembled an old style gypsy, the kind that read your fortunes over a crystal ball.

"Are you kidding? Well, in that case, hop on up. I'll take you for a quick ride and you tell me if you don't wanna get back in the saddle."

"Now?"

"Why not? You don't look like you were going anywhere fast soon."

"But...I don't even know your name."

"Poppy. Yours?"

"Nikki."

"Great! Now we're all introduced, get on and hold tight."

Poppy lifted herself easily up into the saddle and looked expectantly down at me. I took a moment to drink in the sight of this stunning woman smiling down at me, the light blue sky behind her making her seem darker. Then, with a slight struggle, (where I definitely did not look cool) and lots of help from Poppy, I made it up and wrapped my arms around her waist. She smelled of fresh sweat and I caught the scent of citrus shampoo in her hair. It was something I thought I could get very used to.

"Ooh, was it love at first sight?" Amanda interrupted, leaning forward and resting her chin on the palm of her hand. I hesitated for a moment.

"Honestly? I think it was the closest I've ever gotten to love at first sight. She made my stomach spin, but in a totally good way, y'know?"

"Mm, yes I do. So what happened? Did you ask her out?"

"No. I was actually too nervous to say very much to her. I mean, when we were riding, we couldn't really talk at all. But when we stopped and I got off..."

"So, Nikki, if you're not doing anything tomorrow, would you like to come out for dinner?" Poppy hesitated before adding, "Y'know, as in on a date. With me."

Her horse, Thunder as she called him, shuffled his hooves nervously, as if in extension of her own nerves. I didn't answer immediately, unable to believe she'd actually asked me when I'd spent almost the whole ride trying to work out a way to invite her out as casually as possible.

"Maybe I got it wrong, but it's okay if you don't want to, I just..."

"No! I mean yes! Of course I want to. I'd love to!"

"You would?" She looked uncertain for a second, as if she'd been expecting me to say no and that I was just kidding around by saying yes.

"Definitely."

"Oh. Wow." She laughed, looking amused. "I've never asked a complete stranger out on a date before. It went a lot easier than I thought it would."

"I've never been invited out to dinner by a complete stranger either. It felt good."

There was a meeting of our eyes, and our smiles faltered a little as we drained the surrounding area of electricity to scorch back and forth between us. It was intense.

"Sounds like love at first sight to me," Amanda chirped knowingly.

"I swear, I actually felt every single hair on my body stand on end. And I could tell she was feeling it too," I said, rubbing my arms as the same sensation swept over me at the memory.

"I'm just dying to know what happened!"

After we'd swapped numbers and arranged for her to pick me up from home the next evening, Poppy had galloped off into the sunset. I then spent the next twenty-four hours in a state of constant agitation, thinking about her and picturing how our night would go. I spent a lot of time wondering if we were going to end up sleeping together on our first date, but also where we could go for our second, third and fourth dates. For the seven hours leading up to her picking me up, I started working on a new piece which, surprise, bore more than a canny semblance to her.

She turned up on time in a big, rusty old truck and I noticed her pleased appraisal of my choice of clothing, which was one hundred percent reciprocated. She was wearing cowgirl boots, a denim mini skirt and white vest with a cowgirl hat. It was like watching my dream fantasy come to life before my very eyes.

We made polite conversation as she drove us into town, both of us clearly feeling nervous but relaxing slowly and easily in each other's company. By the time she parked up, we were laughing at some silly thing she'd said and I got out of her truck with a smile on my face.

Looking over at Poppy as she shut her door, she smiled back at me. It was the kind of smile that was open and warm and held a lot of promise, the kind I could happily fall in love with, and I held her eye contact, enjoying her attention on me. I was really looking forward to getting to know her.

That was my last thought before, out of nowhere, a car slammed into Poppy and she flew through the air, landing on the tarmac in a horrific tangled mess.

I put my head in my hands to hide the tears. This was the first time I'd relived the accident in full since it had happened, always managing to divert my thoughts before getting to the point of impact. I heard Amanda get up and the next minute her arms were around me and I buried my head in her chest. It wasn't quite the way I had planned to get my head in her chest, but I felt only comfort from it now.

"It was the...the...oh fuck. The sound she made...and the blood on her..." I sobbed, knowing I'd never tell this story again, and needing to get it out.

"Oh, you poor thing. Was it instant?" Amanda soothed, stroking my hair.

"Yeah, I think so. That's wh...what the d...doctors said."

"Then she died happy, and there's no better way to die than that, honey."

"Mom? What's going on?"

We both pulled apart, surprised to find Ness stood watching us with a frown. I quickly tried to hide my face and wipe away the tears that were still flowing from my eyes, feeling embarrassed at being caught in such an intimate situation.

"Oh, hey sweetie. Nothing, we were just chatting about something that happened to Nikki, that's all. Good session?"

"Yeah. Do you want me to go...?"

"No, I'm good." I said, forcing a smile. Ness looked so awkward it fuelled my embarrassment further and I wondered if I'd ever be able to face her again.

The journey home in the car was filled with Amanda talking happily about nonsense, and I could tell she was just trying to lighten the mood. However, Ness couldn't get out of the car fast enough when we'd parked and I deliberately took my time unbuckling.

"Hey, Nikki? Don't mind Ness. I'm sorry she interrupted us."

"No, it's fine."

There was a pause.

"Could I come over later and look at some of your work?"

I looked at her, thinking. I usually didn't like people coming into my studio, home to lots of unfinished pieces, disastrous abandoned pieces I couldn't bring myself to dump, pieces I wasn't quite sure about.

"Sure. Just come straight round the back and knock. I'll be in there all day."

"Great. I'll see you later."

She leaned over and gave me a long warm hug. It felt nice. Really nice.

She didn't come over until early evening, and even though I'd been expecting her to knock, I still jumped when it came. I opened the door, trying to steady my shaking hands.

"Hey. Come on in."

"Sorry I'm a bit late. Got caught up with house rearrangements," she said apologetically as she came in, passing me a pack of beers. "Hope you like beer?"

"Who doesn't? Thanks!"

We opened two and took long appreciative swigs, then I gave her a brief tour of my studio and some of the better ones I was working on. She showed genuine interest which made me feel warm inside.

"Would you do me a commission piece?" She asked, her eyes scoping over the paintings I'd deemed good enough to hang on the wall, my personal favourites.

"Of course. What would you like?"

A smile played at the corner of her mouth as she leaned forward to study some small detail on one.

"I'd like you to paint me. Naked."

I swallowed, hoping she wasn't joking but sure she must be.

"I normally wear clothes when I paint, but I reckon I could make an exception for you."

She laughed and turned to face me.

"I obviously meant myself. It's something I've always wanted to do but wanted to find the right artist and I think you have a remarkable eye for the intimate detail. Have you ever painted anyone nude before?"

"Uh, no." I shook my head emphatically as nerves and adrenaline and lust surged through me, all fighting for pole position. Intimate detail? *Her* intimate detail?

"Would you like to?"

I nodded, not wanting to betray myself by opening my mouth and shouting "Hell, yes!" Amanda leaned back against my work bench and drank some beer, holding eye contact. What was happening here? Was she flirting with me?

"Nikki? The answer's yes."

"Huh?"

"If you're thinking about kissing me."

Okay, I wasn't about to let that invitation slip by. I forced my legs to take shaky steps toward her, feeling her eyes bore seductively into me. I wasn't sure when this sudden change had happened and how had I missed it, but the intensity of what was passing between us was incredibly arousing. I put my beer on the table behind her and she followed suit with her own. Then I placed my hands lightly on her hips and pulled us together, relishing every moment of it and storing it to memory for replay later.

She was still smiling at me, amused by my nervousness it seemed, so I raised an eyebrow before changing tactic. I brought up my right hand and grabbed a handful of her hair before kissing her as passionately and seductively as I could. She responded, pushing her tongue into my mouth and pulling my body tight against her own, a winning combination that made me instantly wet and throbbing. I snuck my knee between hers and wiggled it slightly to open them up, a technique that ensured we could grind ourselves on each other's thighs. Her hand dropped to my ass and she squeezed as she pulled my lower half into her, biting my lip gently as she did. We kissed and ground away on each other for a while, teasing and enjoying each other until, caught up in the spontaneity of the situation, I hoisted her up to sit on my workbench, unsure what she was sitting on and totally not caring. She wrapped her legs around me, and the kissing resumed, hot and lustful and deep. My hand found her left breast and I gave it a firm squeeze, pinching the nipple testily. She gasped, then groaned which told me she liked it hard and passionate, and another wave of wetness flooded round my swollen clit at this thought. But then she suddenly pulled her mouth away from mine, breathing heavily as she watched me.

"What? Did I go too fast?" I asked, regretting my daring nipple move now.

"No, you're fine. But I didn't come over here to have sex with you Nikki, and if we continue, I think that's what's going to happen" she said carefully.

"Oh. Shit. Sorry." I tried to pull away, blushing crimson at having misread everything, but she held onto me.

"Whoa, hold on. I didn't say I don't want to have sex with you. Just not tonight. Is that okay?"

I nodded stupidly at her, studying the way her pupils had dilated in her eyes, the flush of desire on her cheeks, her swollen lips. I felt intoxicated, but the artist in me wanted to note every single detail on her face. She smiled and nodded slowly at me.

"Good. Well, I guess I'd better go." I stepped back to allow her to slide off the bench. "Let me know when you have time to do my painting and we'll talk price then."

"Sure, I'll do that for sure."

"Thanks. I'll see you soon," she said, leaning forward for one last soft, but lingering kiss, and then she walked out of my studio leaving me breathless and more than a little turned on. I braced my hands against the bench, noting one of our beers had been knocked over and was seeping into a pile of rags, but didn't move to clean it up. Amanda's ass had knocked that beer, while we were making out. It was a work of art all in itself.

Then my eyes caught sight of the time.

"Ah shit!" I cursed, suddenly alert and needing to make a decision. Risk running indoors and not making it to my room in the three minutes I had before 'sleep' took over, or staying out here in my studio. The latter won out, and I had a camp bed in the corner specifically for times like this.

As I laid back, one of my last thoughts before I went was wondering what Amanda would have thought if I'd fallen asleep on her mid-kiss?

CHAPTER SIX

It feels like it has taken years to reach this point in my life, although I think it's only been a matter of months. Or it has been months that feel like years.

There was a day once, long ago, when everything went wrong and sent walls caving in around me. Inside those walls were worlds, worlds that live on.

I inhaled and filled my lungs full of smoke, holding it there for pleasurable seconds before I blew out, calming myself with exhalation. I looked around my pathetic flat that I called home. It's just a big room with a bed in a corner and a kitchen area in another, but in between is a wall of windows that I love to stand at, looking out at the city before me.

There is always someone walking past. Sometimes, it's a man who talks on his mobile phone. Other times, it's a woman who smiles. I imagine that she is on her way to meet her lover and the anticipation is spreading across her face from the pleasure she knows he will give her. Or perhaps she is going to buy a chocolate muffin.

All these people and all these lives, on their way to where they have to go and I have nothing better to waste my time with than wondering about days that do not belong to me and are more interesting than mine.

I brought my left hand behind me and fetched out the piece of paper Mr Chan had given me with Helena's address typed on it. The words had not disappeared as I expected and I re-folded the page, returning it to the resting place in my jeans pocket.

Will I get her tomorrow?

I am scared to be where tomorrow may take me. Who goes to sleep at night secure that all will be the same when they next open their eyes? My life can change in the blink of an eyelid.

My life is fragile like love.

In my hand, I let an egg drop and, as the shell splits spewing its contents, all I can feel is the slit that shreds my heart in two. All my love has come tumbling out and there has to be someone to scoop me up and put me back together again.

I walk over to my covered canvas and pull off the sheet, seeing the frame that will make up my image of Freya. As soon as I see my colours, I drift into imagining the soft touch of her skin on mine and immediately feel a tug inside my pants that longs for her fingers. How did she get in when the spectre of Helena has always stood guard at my heart to see off any challenge?

Every wall has a weak point and every piece of armour has a chink. Arrogance shields and blinds eyes from seeing what can be let loose. I have given up fighting because I have been overtaken by lust and it's not all that bad.

I lit up a cigarette, staring at the beginning of a masterpiece, alternating my eyes between the world on my canvas and the world outside my windows.

There must be a difference somewhere between what happens in my head and what happens outside the walls that surround me. Perhaps one day I shall open my eyes.

I breathed out smoke circles and watched as they faded away from me. A circle enclosing dreams that drift away as soon as I try to grab them.

It's the life of my story.

It's time for me to go looking for Helena and I take another drag as I enjoy the moment, knowing it will never come again. There will never be another moment when this anticipation is so exquisite and the pain of not knowing is such an untold pleasure.

It's the second before the orgasm starts when you might go back but it's never going to happen because you know what lies ahead. And acceptance brings an avalanche that cannot be stopped.

Allowing the heart to love is allowing for the avalanche and all that it brings. I think I like the snow. I think I want to be covered in it.

I chucked my butt in the sink, absent mindedly running the tap for a few seconds to drown out any fire. It's what I do with my own fires.

I walked over to the corner that housed my bed and lifted my jumper off the floor, where it lay discarded and threw it on, slipping into my boots at the same time. There will be no tip-toeing today. I slammed shut my door behind me as I shuffled down the stairs and I felt my chest swell with pride.

I am me today when I could have been someone else.

I looked at the toes of my boots as I knocked Freya's door with my knuckles because I am used to looking down and not ahead. I imagined that I heard the soft tread of Freya's feet along her hall carpet and counted in my head the steps she would take until she answered the door.

When that moment went by and I was still staring at my feet, I knocked again, knotting my eyebrows with impatience.

I shook my head, laughing to my toe-caps, realising Freya had gone out. She knew I was going today to check out the address Mr Chan had given me and she had deliberately made herself scarce.

I slid my fag packet out my jeans pocket and took one out as I made my way out, beyond Freya's impassive door. This won't be the first time and neither will it be the last. Barriers are nothing when you have the power of your mind.

I strode out into the sunlight of the day, determined as it was to get through the clouds that were forming a wall to prevent it reaching me.

I looked left and I looked right, breathing in the day, letting the growing wind brush against me, not yet bruising but ready to push me in the direction that I needed to go. I follow where I am led, knowing love is the driving force behind my footsteps. And what other point is there really for stepping forward if it is not to face the challenge that love holds before us?

I am not scared. I have been working to this day for years, desperate to locate Helena, so that I could ask all the questions that grew on top of each other to form a mountain of words in my head, strangling any real speech in me.

As I walked, the questions floated around my head, tormenting me and I began to hum the lyrics to a song that also tormented me. The songs that torment me are the songs that live on forever.

I sat on the 'Clockwork Orange' singing to myself.

My fingers were strumming against my thigh, as I sang the words louder, losing myself in the music. Life is all about losing yourself. If not, how would you know when you are found? I was poked in the ribs by the irate passenger beside me and I shut up then, mouthing an apology I did not mean.

Insincere words are easy for me to say.

How could it be that Helena was at the other end of the same city as me? I have pounded the streets in search…No, I've not. I've stayed in my apartment, scared to venture out because if I bumped into her, I would have to face my fears when I was unarmed. I'm ready now. I'm prepared to hear her say she no longer loves me but I'll never believe it.

As I walked, I thought back to days gone by, when Helena and I were held together in the spider web of love. I feel the trail of her fingertips down my cheeks, held in the grip of her brown eyes.

"I love you," she said.

I panted with the love surging through me. "I know."

"No," she said. "You'll only know when you don't have me."

"I'll always have you," I told her, confident in the power of my adolescent love.

I was reminded of her words, as I held my phone in front of me, walking the paths I was commanded by Google Maps, at once in tune with my heart.

Without realising, my hands had grown clammy, my phone slipping every now and then, as I periodically wiped my hands down the front of my jeans. I exhaled, realising I had been holding my breath, looking up to see my glorious sun surrounded and overtaken by the grey clouds that owned my skies.

I begin to curse as I felt the first spits of rain, memorising the last two roads before I shut off my phone and rammed it into my pocket.

I am almost there. In five minutes I will be upon Helena's house, where she sleeps and laughs and maybe thinks of me once in a while. Today, after ten long years, I will walk back into her life again and hope that welcoming arms will hold me to her.

Where have I gone in ten years? What have I done? What have I achieved?

Ingenting.

The years roll behind me in an avalanche that I am incapable of stopping, try as I might to stand in the way of Time. I will never get those ten years back.

I was twenty when it all went wrong. I am thirty now. Those years are gone, as I edge my way toward my death.

I want my life back.

I want to write my own life instead of looking back on it, having slid away from me when I am too old to feel happiness.

The rain is wetting me in fat, heavy blobs as I finally saw the number of Helena's house amongst the row of impeccable terraced houses. I stood watching through the iron railings that sat on the metre high wall, to keep out the riffraff such as me.

And then I saw her.

A spectre, passing by the window, but I knew immediately it was her. It was Helena, twenty feet away, separated only by rain and brick.

It's now or never. I am not brazen like Nikki, I like to protect myself and keep my heart to myself, not give it away like clothing pegs. But Helena has my heart, she always has and I need this moment. Just a moment to remember those empty years, a wasteland where love could not blossom.

My feet found the way before my head did and before I could control my body, my hand was pressing the bell. I heard the ringing at the back of my mind. It sounded like a hospital alarm.

The door opened.

Helena's eyes met mine.

"Nicosia Poppadoppaluss," she whispered, remembering the pet name she had called me.

"Helena Poppadoppalussanuss," I replied, giving the correct answer.

She ran to me, taking my face in her hands and kissing me. "Nick!"

"Hell."

"Get in," she said, pulling me in from the rain. "You're soaked. Come in here," she said, as I followed. "I'll put the fire on to warm you. Sit here," she went on, pulling over a pouffe. "I'll go make tea."

I shivered in front of her gas fire, feeling my hunger and my cold. I threw my eyes around the room and saw the photos of Helena with a man.

She came back in the room as I scowled at one in particular: her wedding photo.

"Drink this tea," she said.

I took the warm cup, wordlessly.

"You've lost weight," she said.

"You've put on some," I retorted.

She laughed uneasily. "I'm expecting a baby." I felt horror as her hands unconsciously went to her stomach.

"You couldn't wait for me?" I asked.

"Nick, it's been ten years…"

"You said you'd wait forever," I interrupted.

"I was twenty. I've grown up now."

"Because you're married?" I said, unkindly because I was feeling hard done by. I don't know what I honestly expected but it had not been finding Helena pregnant and married to a man.

"You left me!" she shouted. "What did you think I'd do? Pine myself to death? Don't think you're better than me because you're a martyr and I'm a realist!"

"I left you?" I tried to find a memory but my mind rebelled against me.

"Yes, Nick. Don't you remember? I told you I'd love you forever and I meant that. I still love you but I have learned to live without you. That's what people do, they move on."

"You still love me?" I stood up and walked over to her. She'd cut her hair. It no longer curled off her shoulder blades but sat on top in a straight bob, those wayward curls having been defied. "I never stopped loving you," I said, when my lips were centimetres from hers.

I felt her breath on my face. It was a warm wind that caressed me back into the palm of her hand. "Why didn't you phone me?" I asked.

She gave me a look, as if I did not know who I was. "Don't you recall? Are you forgetting you abandoned me?"

"I abandoned you?" I repeated with the horror running through me.

Her deep brown eyes caught me and I saw the film of tears grow over as the memories caught up with her. She touched my cheek with her hand.

"When I needed you, you were nowhere," she said, softly.

"I have never been anywhere that didn't involve you," I answered.

She brought her face to mine and kissed me. I closed my eyes but the fireworks deserted me.

"Vakker kjaerlighet," I whispered, beyond myself.

Helena pulled away. "What did you say there?"

"I don't know," I admitted, struggling to pull together the voice that had whispered those words to me.

"Nick, I had glandular fever. For three months I reached out to you and you never came."

I stuttered. "I never changed my phone number."

"My phone broke. My parents got me a new one, I didn't have your number."

"You knew where I lived," I pouted.

"Oh, I should chase after you after I've been ill in bed for months and you can't be bothered to see me?"

"I came every day to your door."

"My parents would have told me," she said.

"Did they?"

"No," she said.

"Then they lied," I told her, turning away, throwing my hand across the wedding photo so that it would fall to the ground and break. "Who the fuck is he anyway?"

"My husband?" she said, almost apologetically.

"No, fucking Willy Wonka."

She gave me that look where her dark eyes smouldered. A look that, when I was a teenager, would have shot me down. "He's a good man."

I guffawed and immediately regretted it, as I saw her defences go up. Once upon a time, those defences would have been to protect me. I quickly saw that her loyalties now lay with other legs between hers.

"Drommer," I scoffed.

I saw the shade of red work up from her shoulder blades to her throat and up her cheeks. "You come to my home and still think you are better than me? Look at you: jeans full of holes, boots that are scuffed to death and a jumper that's holier than the Pope. You don't even have a coat!"

"I don't need a coat to love someone!" I shouted back.

"Love isn't fancy words and half-painted canvasses, Nick!"

"And what does Mr Husband do?" I said, pretending to be a peacock, strutting. "Oh, I look after Mrs Wife," I mimicked.

"Edmund Nightingale is the manager of 'Marks & Sparks' in the West End."

I fell into a fit of laughter. "Manager at 'Marks & Sparks'? That's what I've been thrown over for?"

I saw the rage on Helena's face but I've seen her rage before and it didn't scare me. Only one thing scares me really.

"You left me!" she said, fuming closer into my face.

"I never left you," I said. I gave up then and put my lips on hers, where they belonged, trying to remember the taste of her and how our lips moved together, how our bodies pressed against each other.

All I knew was the touch of ice upon me.

Where was my Helena who used to fill me with such longing I was fit to burst? I kissed her harder, feeling no resistance, and wrapped my arms around her tight. Where once there was fire, there now was glaciers.

Isbre.

I felt the tickle of tears gliding down my cheek and I opened my eyes, pulling back to see the unhappiness leaking from Helena.

"You broke my heart!" she screamed at me, pushing me away.

"No, no, Helena, you broke mine. I've been waiting all this time for you to mend it."

She wiped at her face savagely, smoothing away her tears. "So you've been a nun, eh? Who else have you slept with?"

I took a step back, stunned by the venom in her words, so quickly after a moment of tenderness but doesn't tenderness always breed resentment?

"I…I…," I faltered.

Her face snarled, her lips curling tight over her teeth. "How many, Nick?"

My head started to pound, faces swirled around as I struggled to hold on to where this gravity grounded me, hearing "How many? How many, Nick?" over and over again.

"I've had…some…other lovers. Poppy…no, I had Malena…fuck."

"There's two already."

"I can count!" I shouted. "There was Jude and Evie, ah fuck."

"Up to four now, keep going."

I screwed my eyes shut tight. I couldn't tell who I had been with, who was mine or who was Nikki's, that bitch on heat that fucked anything in a skirt.

"Freya. I made love to Freya," I blurted and thinking of Norwegian passion calmed me. In the toss of a coin, my mind was quiet. I would need to take a minute later to consider why this should be so.

"Five? Finished or going higher?" Helena asked.

"It doesn't matter, Helena. We weren't together and I had needs, just as you obviously did," I told her sadly, resigned to the wasteland of years that lay between our meetings.

"Look, you'll have to go now. Edmund's mother is coming to take me buggy shopping. Leave me your number. I promise I'll call." She smiled but her smile no longer dissolved me.

She handed me her phone and I tapped my details into her contacts folder. "I'm sorry, Helena. I had this meeting so differently in my head but I'm a dreamer, I always have been. I just, oh I don't know, longed for a happy ending."

"Maybe our ending has not yet been written," she said, filling my battered heart with hope.

For the first time, I looked into her eyes and gave her a proper smile. I put my hand on her shoulder and squeezed. "Until next time."

I left, closing her door behind me, determined not to look back lest I see her reflection watching me and I ran back in. I kept walking back down the row of terraced houses, feeling my legs grow weaker and weaker, finally buckling under the torrential rain when I was out of her sight. I let myself fall to my knees, caving in to the maelstrom of emotions creating a tornado in my mind.

I touched Helena!

She was there, in front of me, in my arms, kissing me. She said she still loved me but she was married and about to have a baby in a few months. I ran my fingertips across my brow, back and forth, a habit I had when the thoughts behind it became almost too much, like ironing out the creases would straighten my mind.

I was unravelling. I felt my heart break in two, all the love inside pouring out before onto the puddled pavement. I heard my choked sobs before I realised I was crying and threw my hands over my face, hiding my shame. The rain pelted my neck and soaked my newly dried clothes but all I could think about was that I no longer knew where I belonged. For ten years, I had held on to love in the form of Helena and now I would need to let go and I couldn't bear it. I couldn't let my love for her fizzle out like a match under a tap.

Then God sent an angel to rescue me.

"Be still," I heard and my heart began to calm. Strong arms lifted me to standing and I was being shushed.

"You should have waited for me," she said.

"You weren't in," I said to Freya.

"Quick. To my car we run," she said, grabbing my hand and pulling me to where we could shelter from the rain.

"You weren't in," I repeated, shaking my hair dry like a dog.

"My best friend, Mavis Street, had a medical emergency. I had to attend on her and keep illness from her. I tried to get back in time but you'd left me already. Now I am straight here while I buy soup."

"Soup?"

"Yes, it's Tuesday. On Tuesday, Mavis Street will only eat soup."

"Any particular type of soup or is she not fussy?" I said, playing along.

"Tomato. She has her ways but now, my Nick, give me your hands. I take your bruised heart and smooth the path to Freya," she smiled, taking my hands in hers and rubbing them warm.

Oddly, I did feel the cold lift, my fractured heart began to knit back together and I drowned in the mesmerising blue of Freya's eyes.

"Later you will tell me about Helena. First we go to Mavis Street and you will dry off." She beamed a smile at me. "I'll take you and caress my light into your dark, don't worry."

And I didn't worry. My mind had emptied and I let the windscreen wipers hypnotise me, as they flicked back and forth, until we pulled up outside a quirky, little house set back along a path in a lake.

"Who lives here?" I joked. "Bilbo Baggins?"

Freya frowned at me. "Be kind, Nick. Mavis Street is a dwarf."

I swallowed my embarrassment as curiosity overtook me. I was privately pleased to be allowed a glimpse into Freya's hidden world and interested as to why her best friend would be a dwarf. I knew Freya did have a secret because some nights before sleep claimed me, I'd hear her door banging shut as she leapt out into the night.

Intrigued, I followed her into Mavis' house, hit by a wall of hot air as the door closed behind me.

"I am back, Mavis Street," Freya said, loudly. "I have my lover, Nick, with me."

I cringed a bit at her calling me her lover. We hadn't established that yet and I still had to figure out where Helena's return would fit into my life. If at all.

"I'm in the kitchen," I heard a low voice answer back.

Freya nodded her head toward the kitchen and I followed her in, seeing the dwarf woman in her dwarf kitchen fetching a bowl from a cupboard that might have been too high for her had the room not been made in miniature.

"Did you bring the soup?" she asked Freya, then seeing me she beamed broadly, with her slightly lopsided mouth. "You must be the lover."

"Hmm-mmm," I replied, non-committal, looking around the room, fascinated and feeling like a giant.

"I'm so pleased to finally meet you, Nick. I have heard lots about you, that you paint. I'd love you to paint me, I'll pay. Oh, look at my tongue rushing away. Allow me to introduce myself: I am Mavis Street and I have an enlarged heart."

"Hello, Mavis Street," I said, unable to conceal my amusement. It was one of those surreal days that feels like a puppet-master is pulling all the strings and I have to travel the directions I am thrown down.

"Mavis Street is my best friend," Freya said.

"You already told me that," I pointed out.

"You'll be our best friend, too," Mavis Street said.

"I will?" I questioned, my lips curling into a smile.

Mavis Street met my eyes. "Oh, yes."

"You're a freak like us," Freya added.

I would have laughed but any laughter gargled a death in my throat as I regarded Freya and Mavis. As alike as sausages and cheese.

Freya with her beautiful blue eyes, white hair that fell down her back like an ice-cap and a figure that made me ache under her nifty, home-made dresses.

Mavis Street: dwarf with an enlarged heart and lopsided lips; with a head too large and hair too curly; a brown eye and a green eye; a nose that was flattened by imaginary punches; wearing clothes that held the tell-tale signs of Freya's sewing skills to fit her snugly. Mavis Street was ugly but there was something in her low voice that made me think she might be the most beautiful person in the whole world. She had the voice of honey love.

"She knows," Mavis said, turning her back on me, taking the cans of soup from the carrier bag Freya had lain on the table. "Would you like some tomato soup, Nick?"

Suddenly, I was ravenous and I nodded, licking my lips as my taste buds itched on my tongue. Freya pulled a chair out at the small table and I crouched down to sit and await the food, while Freya and Mavis heated the soup and buttered some bread.

I grabbed a piece of bread and hungrily began to eat, reaching greedily for the first bowl of hot soup and burning myself as I spooned in the hot, orange liquid.

"She's a one," Mavis said to Freya, regarding me.

Freya smiled proudly. "She's my one," she said, as I ate.

"I'm here, you know," I managed between gulps.

When I'd finished eating, Mavis came over and gave me a card. She said, "If ever you need a job, you call me."

I looked at the card. It said 'Mavis Street: Dwarf Adventurer'.

"Thanks," I said, scraping my chair along the floor as I stood up. "I have to get home," I told Freya.

As I walked to her car, I heard the honeydew voice remind me, "I meant what I said about you painting me."

I threw my hand up in a wave of acknowledgement but I was growing tired, my eyelids heavy with the strain of the day and I needed my bed. I sat quietly, lost in myself before the curtain of black would descend on me.

"I'll sleep alone," I told Freya, as I climbed the stairs to my flat. I felt her eyes on my back but I was too exhausted to face her and I almost fell in my door, managing to lock it behind me.

I should have let sleeping dogs lie, I thought, as I flung my clothes off into a corner and dropped onto my mattress.

There was one sleeping dog I'd like to die.

CHAPTER SEVEN

If there was one thing that confused me more than my *situation,* it was women. For example, I hadn't had any attention from any women for the last couple of years and had kind of thrown myself into my art work instead. Now I was struggling to keep track of how many were interested in me.

This was exactly what I was thinking when I looked outside my studio window and saw Malena skulking nervously outside, obviously unaware she was being watched and chewing on a fingernail as she contemplated her next move. Frowning, I wiped my fingers clean on a dirty rag (well, smudged the oils into the creases of my fingers to be more precise) and headed to the door.

"Malena? What's up?"

She jumped guiltily and stared at me like a rabbit caught in headlights.

"Oh! Hey, I wasn't sure...how you doin' Nick?"

"It's Nikki, not Nick." *I'm nothing like that psycho.* "I'm okay. You?"

"Yeah, good."

The atmosphere was about as awkward as it could get as we both stared each other down. I noted she had her t-shirt on inside out, but bit my lip against pointing it out.

"Was there something I could help you with?" I prompted.

"I...can I come inside?"

"Sure." I stepped back and she hesitantly shuffled past me into my studio where the awkwardness intensified. I had to resist the urge to run around covering all my work, especially as she didn't seem at all interested in any of it.

"So I'm not...I'm not like you."

Oh no.

"That's okay. Everyone's different, right?"

She gulped and I swallowed, hoping she wasn't aiming where I thought she was.

"I need to know. I need to understand...I mean, I kissed you first. What does that mean?"

"It doesn't mean anything other than you were confused..."

"You're right!" she interrupted, moving to stand in front of me. I held my ground, not wanting to offend her by stepping back. "I am confused, Nick."

"Nikki" I growled, hating how even in denial at being compared to *her*, I sounded like her.

"I can't stop thinking about it. About you," she admitted, looking like a lost lamb. I idly wondered how many other cute animals one person could resemble. I sighed, trying not to look into her Poppy-like eyes lest the day-nightmares resume. Also, she was extremely hot, and I was still a red blooded lesbian at the end of the day.

"You will. It's just your mind's way of distracting you from...well, you know."

I wasn't actually prepared for her launching herself at me, lips puckered and tasting of smoke from a recent cigarette, which is why I took so long to respond (although red blooded lesbian inside me might have had more than a little sway in the delay) but I tried as tactfully as possible to extract myself from her. When I'd succeeded, her face crumpled and she turned away from me quickly.

"Why don't you want me? Aren't I good enough? Was Pop prettier, huh?"

I swallowed thickly, glad this wasn't Nick dealing with this particular problem — she would have been likely to just tell her to fuck off and get over herself or something.

"No, it's not that. Oh man, you kinda remind me a little too much of Poppy, y'know? When I look at you...I just see her." This was as close to the truth as I was willing to go and I was quite proud of myself for finding a way that wouldn't completely hurt her frayed emotions anymore. Until she turned around.

"So you *do* want me?"

"Um..."

Unable to lie on the spot, because there was indeed a very horny part of me that did want her, I just ended up staring at her helplessly. She took advantage of my hesitancy and stepped forward again.

"Look, it's okay. I broke up with Brad yesterday. It's not like I'd be cheating on him or anything."

"You had a boyfriend?"

"I couldn't stop thinking about you. Do you...do you think when Pop died, she, y'know...d'you think a part of her soul came into me?"

"Oh Malena, please go home and think about this properly."

"I'm not confused!" She shouted. "Well, I am, but not about how I feel about you, Nick!"

"I'M NOT FUCKING NICK!"

And as if possessed by my counterpart, I shoved her with all my might, sending her flying back onto my desk.

Well, after that it seemed only right to have sex with her to make up for being such a bastard.

*** *** ***

After Malena had left (with a nervous promise to call me soon) I knew I wouldn't be getting any more work done, so I headed into the house for an update on Amanda from mom. This was handy, especially since I didn't even need to ask for it, and it satisfied my nosey curiosity about what they were all getting up to.

"Nikki, they've just had a big delivery turn up on the back of a truck," Mom whispered excitedly as I walked into the house. "Did they say they were expecting anything when you were out with them yesterday?"

"Did it look like an altar?"

I laughed as mom's head turned slowly to look at me, mouth hanging open in shock.

"Mum, I'm just kidding. No, they didn't mention to me what they might be getting delivered. But I'm willing to bet it's something perfectly normal. And un-occult-ish. Listen, I think I'm going to go out for a wee while, want me to get anything fir ye?"

Mom frowned at me, looking puzzled.

"What? Did I say something weird?"

"Why are you talking in a Scottish accent?"

I stopped, feeling my blood freeze. Had I? Was I?

"I gotta go," I mumbled, hearing even in my own ears the Celtic-ness struggling to break through. I ignored mom (had I called her mum?) and ran to the door, grabbing my helmet and keys. I needed to ride, and ride fast.

I literally span the wheels in my haste to gun away quickly, and nearly peed my pants as the front end lifted slightly, threatening to throw me onto my back. But I managed to keep some tenuous control, and almost sighed as I put some distance between mom and myself. Of course, I knew mom wasn't what I was running from, but everyone knew you couldn't run from yourself. Damn Nick! How dare she leak through into my world, into *me*! I don't know how she managed it, but it wasn't funny. I could practically hear that cruel laugh of hers in my head, mocking me as she no doubt felt mighty proud of her accomplishment.

I tugged on the throttle, pushing my speed up past levels I was comfortable with until I was too scared to take my eyes off the road to even check how fast I was going. It was terrifying, but not nearly as much as the thought of turning into Nick.

A figure in the distance caught my eye, strange because it was such a scorching hot day and they were heading seemingly nowhere. I braked, glad of the distraction, and prepared myself to offer them help. Taking in their bare feet, dirty white shirt and faded jeans as I got closer, I deduced that it was possibly a young male in his early twenties. Although definitely not a cowboy, he walked with enough purpose that said he knew where he was going. Now I wanted to stop and help more to quench my curiosity than anything else and as I coasted up to him, he heard me slowing down and turned.

Yup. The sun had gone to town on him, and I sucked in a breath as his almost comically bright red face looked at me, puzzled as to why I had stopped.

"Are you okay? Do you need directions or anything?" I shouted over the noise of the engine.

"No, you're good. I know where I'm going."

He tried to smile, but the tight skin on his cheeks prevented it from filling out properly. Glad he couldn't see me grimacing behind my helmet, I pushed on.

"Well, can I give you a lift? You look like the sun's caught you out a little there."

"No, I need to do this journey by foot. Otherwise he won't see me."

"Who won't see you?"

"The Indian. You have to walk to him with no food or water, or he won't see you."

I turned off my bike and removed my helmet, fully intrigued.

"What Indian? And how do you know where he is? There's nothing out this way but sand and dust."

"Oh, he's out here. The directions are to walk out of town past the burnt out tree, then walk towards the ten o'clock sun until you hit a trio of rocks. From there, you have to use your intuition about which way to go, cos he never stays in one place. People say it's the Earth that shifts, not him," he added conspiratorially.

"Can I join you?" I found myself asking. I didn't expect him to say yes, to be honest, but he nodded happily. He waited patiently for me to remove my leathers and helmet, stashing them with my bike out of view of the road before we started walking.

We made small talk for a while, but it dried up along with the saliva in my mouth and we continued the journey in an awkward kind of comfortable silence. I used the time to think about what I was going to ask the Indian (if he actually existed) and to hope he was well stocked up on food and water. I wondered if getting fed was part of the deal? In fact, I wondered what exactly the 'deal' was? All I knew was that this felt right, like I was supposed to be doing this, for whatever reason that may be. Perhaps this Indian could give me some answers.

After a while, we found the burnt out tree and I checked my watch. It was nearly eleven. Could an hour really make that much difference to the position of the sun? Without discussing it, we both came to a mutual decision about which way to head and carried on. By now, I was starting to feel pretty dehydrated and I wondered how he was managing. Plus, my pale skin was not liking the intense unwavering heat, and I was on the verge of quitting and heading back to my bike when we saw the trio of rocks in the distance. Having come this far, I decided to just carry on, if not so I could at least rehydrate myself before attempting the journey back in the unforgiving midday sunshine.

But when we reached the rocks, we both stopped. I remembered his words — to trust our intuition for which way to go, and now we seemed kind of stuck. I tried to summon some moisture into my mouth, but even my eyeballs felt dry. In fact, I'd happily have licked his if I thought there was any kind of fluid on them, and been more than willing to share my own eye juice with him. Had I had any, that is.

Mr Red (I couldn't remember the name he'd told me and had this nickname in my head now) made to shuffle off to the right, but something made me touch his arm and stop him. I shook my head and continued to walk in the same direction we had been to get here, not caring if he followed me – I was on my own mission now. His gentle barefooted steps behind me confirmed he was trusting my intuition over his own, for whatever good it would do.

Yet after over an hour and a half of seeing nothing but rocks, dirt and foliage, my heart began to do a worried jig in my chest. What if we didn't find him? How would we describe where we were to the emergency services, and what reason could we possibly have for pulling such a reckless stunt and needing rescuing?

I stopped walking. Enough was enough. Our lives were at risk now. I turned around to tell Red, and that was how I saw it. In fact, if I hadn't stopped where I did, when I did, we probably would have walked straight on by without seeing it, but see it I did. Goosebumps raised on my scorched arms.

Over to our right there was a small dip in the landscape, and just poking out of the top of the dip was the tip of a teepee. I started walking towards it, hoping this was real and not some kind of mirage created by my hopeful mind, but it just got more real the closer we got.

There was a young woman in her mid twenties smoking a cigarette on a stool outside, and I got the impression she'd been expecting us as she didn't look at all surprised to see two straggly visitors rocking up. If anything, she seemed mightily pissed off. Her long dark hair looked as if it had just been freshly washed and styled, and her plain shirt and jeans fresh on. I wondered how she could look so neat and tidy in such a dusty, wild environment.

Red found some last reserves of energy as we neared and got to her before me, falling to his knees in front of her. She rolled her eyes, unimpressed.

"I'm here to see the Indian. I followed all of the rules, just like I was supposed to," he rasped, and my eyes watered at how dried out he sounded. Shaking her head as if he'd totally irritated her, she finished her smoke and stubbed it out angrily.

"Follow me." She glanced at me, curiously. "Not you. Wait there."

Then they both disappeared into the large (and no doubt deliciously cool) teepee, leaving me wondering what I was supposed to do. There wasn't anywhere to sit, unless I wanted to poach the woman's chair, so I sat on the ground with my back against the fabric and rested my eyes while I waited.

"Here, drink this. Slowly, otherwise you'll cramp up." I started guiltily as the woman had silently returned and was offering me a roughly carved wooden cup filled with fluid I assumed was water. Her expression had altered dramatically and I couldn't help but stare at the kind and compassionate lady before me as I took a well needed swig from the cup. As it flowed gloriously down my dry throat, I was startled to find the liquid inside wasn't water after all, more a sweet and beautifully soothing elixir of some sort. I tried my best not to chug it back, but the cup was empty all too soon.

"Thank you," I practically whispered, overcome with gratitude.

"You're welcome. I have some cream inside for your skin, so you won't burn." She watched me, a small smile playing on her lips. "So where'd you pick that joker up?" She asked, hooking her thumb towards the teepee entrance.

"I saw him walking along the road and just kinda tagged along. Sorry, I hope it was okay for me to turn up?"

"What are you talking about? We've been expecting you! He was never supposed to make it here."

I swallowed, marvelling at how the elixir was still coating my mouth and throat, but puzzled at her words.

"Me? I don't understand."

"Mr Red in there was never going to find us, so he musta tagged along with you. At the rocks?"

I remembered how he had indeed been about to head off in a different direction when I'd stopped him, roughly about the same time I noticed her use of my nickname for him.

"How did you...?"

"That's not important right now. In a few more minutes, we can go on in and do what you came here for."

"What's happening in there?"

"Well, it's kinda complicated. Visitors like you we expect, and know are coming. But there was a time when everyone wanted to come out and see us, with stupid inane questions like is my husband cheating on me, will I get that promotion, am I going to have twins? So we moved a bit further out and made up some rules to be followed in order to be seen by us. Travel by foot from town, no food or water, yada yada yada." She laughed, a wickedly mischievous look on her face. "Now only the 'dedicated' make it out to us, so we get them rehydrated, give them a pokey pipe to smoke, and feed them some peyote. Let them find the answers on their own."

"Isn't that a bit reckless? What if they have an adverse reaction or something?"

She gave me an incredulous look.

"Reckless? These are people who have walked twenty odd miles in blistering heat with no water, I'd say they're pretty reckless already. Anyway, they always go away happy." She shook her head. "Where are my manners? My name's Mina. It's a pleasure to meet you Nicola."

I shook her hand, puzzled.

"My name's Nikki."

"No, honey, it's Nicola," she said softly. "Don't worry, it won't be long before it all gets straightened out."

"Will the Indian give me the answers I need?"

Mina frowned, amused.

"No, he just cooks up the peyote for the others. You don't think you're here to see him do you?"

"I...I don't know."

Everything was starting to feel really surreal and hazy, especially when she took my hand to help me stand.

"It's me that's been waiting to see you. Come on, we can go inside now."

"I feel...weird."

"It's called sleepy. You've never experienced that, have you?"

I yawned, finding it hard to keep my eyes open as we went through the small opening into the dark tent. Mina guided me to a pile of what looked like sheepskins on the floor and indicated that I should sit down, so I sank into the plush softness. It was hard to see anything, but I could tell it was a lot bigger on the inside than it appeared to be on the outside.

"Huh. Like the Tardis," I commented, more to myself.

"I suppose, yes. Nicola, do you remember when you were nine years old?"

"Did you drug me? Was that drink peyote?" I asked, shaking my head against the softness enveloping it.

"No, I didn't drug you, I just have...let's say 'an effect' on people." Mina cocked her head at me, thinking to herself. "Let me get you another drink, then I think it might do you good to talk rather than me asking you questions."

She walked backwards into the darkness so I was unable to see her, despite gazing intently. I felt like I was in the depths of some large cave in a mountain, and restrained myself from shouting out to see if I had an echo, mainly because I wasn't sure how I'd react if there was. Also, it was so black in here, I had to blink to reassure myself my eyes weren't closed. On the floor in front of me was a magazine, and I picked it up, thinking how out of place it seemed in here.

"Here. This is the same as before, so just sip it, okay?"

My eyes snapped open, startling me, and I sat forward breathing heavily.

"What's happening to me?"

"You just drifted off for a few seconds. It happens."

"But, I felt like I was awake!"

"That's what it feels like to dream. You've never experienced dreaming before, have you? Let me ask you something. Do you believe there is anything real outside your perception of reality?"

"What?"

Mina sat on the blankets next to me, and put her arm around my shoulders. It felt kind of safe and I found myself snuggling into the comfort with ease.

"Start at the beginning, and tell me about your life. Not the mundane stuff, the important stuff. The secret stuff."

"You'll think I'm crazy," I whispered, knowing I was going to tell her anyway.

"You are crazy. But I want to hear it from your own mouth."

So I told her. For the first time in my whole life, I told the full unedited version. How I was Nikki for twelve hours of the day, living in Saloam Springs, USA, but every night at exactly the same time, I would close my eyes and wake up as Nick, angry Scot in the UK. We both looked roughly the same, and both loved women, but that was where the similarity ended. Although we shared the same passion for art, I was successful whereas she had failed miserably. Twelve hours in each body, neither able to communicate with the other, nor wanting to.

"Have you ever wondered if this is all real? Or rather, how much of it is real?" Mina asked carefully.

"I used to all the time. But wondering never answered any of my questions so I stopped. Is it real?" I got the feeling she knew more than she was letting on, but wanted me to work it out for myself rather than just tell me.

"Is anything real? Ultimately everything is made up of energy, but it's how we perceive it through our eyes and other senses that makes it 'real' in our minds. You had your first dream a short while ago, and it felt as real as you sat chatting to me now, correct?"

I nodded, frowning.

"So how do you know you're not dreaming now? This feels as 'real' as when you were dreaming, so how can you differentiate between the two experiences?"

My jaw fell open, and I stared at her, completely stumped.

"Am I?"

"Whether you're awake or dreaming, honey, my answer would always be the same. What's more important is to ask if you are really in control."

I felt a hand shaking my arm gently and turned...

...Opening my eyes as I did so.

"Hey, you drifted off for a second there. Here, I brought you some fruit."

I jumped up from the floor as Mina crouched down in front of me, holding out a small bowl containing what looked like mango in bite size cubes.

"No! We were just talking! You were sat down with me and...and...what the fuck is going on?" I cried out, feeling completely out of control. Mina put a gentle hand on my arm, squeezing reassuringly.

"It's ok, calm down honey. Come here," she whispered, pulling me into her arms. I found it hard to breathe and wondered if I was having a panic attack, but allowed her to embrace me only because I needed to feel something solid.

"What's happening here?"

"Whatever is happening to you is what you need to see, or hear, or feel. It's the way it is in here. I can't give you the answers, but you can find them from your experience if you are smart. Some people see what they want to see, or just plain ignore the truth, but that's for them to choose. You've been given the answers, Nicola, choose how to interpret them in whatever way you wish."

"But, I didn't get any answers, just lots of questions."

"If you have the right questions, you'll find the right answers. Ask the wrong ones, and you'll only get sent in the wrong direction." She stiffened, pulling back to look me compassionately in the eye. "Oh dear. I do have something to tell you after all. There will be a lot of death coming your way, and you won't be able to stop any of it so don't try. It's only from the death that you, your true self, can be reborn."

I blinked at her as an icy shiver invaded my nervous system.

"Who? Who's going to die?"

"We're all going to die. When our time comes, it will always be at the right time." Mina stroked a red bang away from my face before kissing my forehead soothingly. "Now it's time for you to go. Your bike is outside and you have just enough time to get home before Nick takes over. Good luck sweetheart."

I opened my eyes and found I was outside the teepee, sat against the canvas in the same position where I'd been when I first got here. I jumped up and ran into the teepee, only to find it empty, and a good deal smaller than how it had been when I'd been in it before. *If* I'd been in it before.

Mina, the Indian and Red were nowhere to be seen.

Running back outside I stopped dead in my tracks — my bike was on its stand waiting for me with my leather jacket and helmet.

I rode home, crying all the way, and when I closed my eyes for Nick's turn, there were still tears falling.

CHAPTER EIGHT

I woke knowing the slut I shared my mind with had been spreading her snail trail again and I stripped myself of my pants and t-shirt as I made my way to shower clean her animal lusts.

Nikki was like a man: ruled by her sex organs.

I snorted and let the warm water cool my hatred.

Helena had kissed me.

It was not Freya's kiss.

Helena was married and having a man's baby.

Helena who had sworn she could never love anyone but me.

My Helena, that I had loved for ten, lonely years was nothing more than a liar, who had fallen with ease down the well-worn path of husband and child.

But I loved her!

Did I? Did I really love her? Could I feel love for someone who let me slip from their life without a fight and never thought to come looking for me, knowing where I lived? Helena had meekly accepted the version of events fed to her by her wealthy, judgemental parents who had never liked me and who disapproved of our love affair.

Everyone disapproved of me except Freya and the woman I called mother.

I had wasted ten years of my life loving a ghost, a woman who existed only in my mind and I began to cry with the injustice and stupidity of it all.

My heart, that I thought so fierce and loyal, was nothing more than an organ of duplicity, tricking me into a loneliness that I surely did not deserve. I had loved Helena and no other. I had not leapt into bed with others, unlike Nikki. I had remained true.

"Until Freya," something whispered.

"Until Freya," I agreed, through my tears that wet my face and were drowned by the water of the shower. Almost like my tears were being washed away.

Helena had kissed me and…

Nothing. *Ingenting.*

Ten years is too long to hold on to passion. And in my darkness, a light had shone in reminding me of the wonder of love and of why I had been so reluctant to let go of what I had once felt.

I stepped out my shower, towelling myself dry, and found a clean pair of pants, clean bra and a t-shirt that declared Joan Jett loved rock and roll.

I found my jeans and boots by the door, where I must have thrown them off in my haste to get to bed, and grabbed my fags, before shutting my door on the snib.

I lit one of my cigarettes, stuffing them into my back pocket, looking at the engraved Zippo. It said: "An end is a beginning." Helena had given it to me when I was sixteen and thought it was cool to smoke. I used to light my smoke, then blow the flame, seeing it waver and wobble in my wind but still it would burn.

"That's my love for you," I'd tell her. "It will always burn."

I looked at the lighter I had re-filled for the last ten years and I huffed, throwing a big breath to the flame.

It died in my wind.

Nothing lasts forever. I thought it would but I was wrong. Flames die out and new passions ignite new flames. If a love is unrequited it is because it is a love that is not meant to be, otherwise it would surely be requited and celebrated because true love always finds a way.

I kicked my heels past Freya's door and made my way outside. The rain had stopped but it was still cold and I wished I had put a jumper on. It wouldn't matter, as I had no intention of being out for long. I quickly made my way to our local park, where I sat on the grass dampening the bottom of my jeans. I picked at the daisies that grew abundantly, deftly stabbing holes in their stalks with a fingernail to thread through another stalk. I made myself a daisy chain and placed it on my head, and sat playing with flowers a moment more.

It wasn't long before I was back at Freya's door, this time stopping to knock. I felt a flutter of nerves in my stomach as I waited for her to pull open her door and greet me with her alluring smile.

"Nick!" she beamed. "Are you coming in? Oh, I love your daisy tiara," she laughed.

She was perfect, I thought, drinking in her image. Her hair was loose and tousled, betraying that I had roused her from a slumber. Her eyes were sleepy but still sparkled with interest and her white silken night-dress clung to her hips and breasts, sending a shiver down my spine that jellied my legs.

"I made one for you," I said, still stood on her doorstep, holding out her daisy chain in my hands, like a sacrificial offering.

She laughed again, happily taking the flimsy flower chain and placing it on her white-blonde hair. It is the simple things that make women smile I have found.

"Thank you, Nick. Come in, please," she said, holding the door wide but not so wide that my body had to slip against hers as I slid past. Our eyes met for an instant and I felt the blush of my passion spill through my cheeks.

The last ten years of my life had been spent in days filled with hatred and anger, and this is what I had become used to. I had been so consumed with Helena leaving me and threw my pain into anger at the world. Around my ears, my world was dissolving and I did not have enough anger now to fight off my feelings. Finally seeing Helena had wiped away the time between and now I felt empty.

Empty ready to be refilled.

I went into Freya's lounge where her sofa was, remembering the last time I had sat there the night she had cooked me dinner. I don't know how long ago that was.

"What is it you are wanting with me, Nick?" Freya asked, padding across her carpet with her bare feet.

"I wanted you to pose for another hour so that I can finish my painting of you. I'll be able to do the rest on my own from memory once I have done a few more bits," I told her.

"I will gladly sit for you," she said, agreeably, standing in front of my sitting form, pushing herself in between my knees a little. A little but enough to send longings throughout me until all I could think of was grabbing her and pressing my lips on her.

"You know, Nick," she said, slowly, looking deep into me with her eyes of blue. "If you want to kiss me, you can."

It was all the invitation I needed. I jumped up, pushing my lips on hers and opening her mouth with my tongue. My hand clasped her neck to keep her tight against me and my remaining hand grabbed her buttock, thrusting her up into me.

Her hands were ripping at my t-shirt, and we separated our lips momentarily as I wriggled it over my head. Her fingers clicked at my bra strap and it fell loose for me to let it fall down my arms and drop to the floor.

I could not take my eyes from hers. She was possessing me.

I kissed her again, slower this time, letting our tongues find a rhythm with our lips curling around each others. I enjoyed the taste of her and savoured it, kissing her harder and holding her closer.

I was overtaken by passion, feeling an explosion in every nerve-ending throughout my body as I felt her hands work my jeans free and she grabbed my buttocks as the denim slipped down my legs.

I jerked with a pang of lust that began in my pants and ran through my body because Freya's fingers had found their way inside and were working me gently.

I gasped and she smiled into my eyes before lowering her mouth to kiss my erect nipple. I closed my eyes as I felt her wet lips touch me and her tongue begin its mesmerising circles.

I was lost to Freya and the touch of her skin on mine and for the next hour, I forgot anything else existed but her.

For that hour, I believe I was truly happy.

Happiness is not an emotion I am familiar with experiencing: it's a watering hole in the oasis of my life; always in the distance within view but out of my grasp. I had gotten so used to my own self-inflicted misery that I had forgotten what it was like to smile and laugh without restraint, to have soft arms around me that held me in their love and eyes that looked on me with passion, not pity.

Lying in Freya's arms, with her naked body draped over mine was the moment, I think, that I began to let my walls down. The moment I realised that I could actually love someone else beyond the obsession I felt for Helena — which wasn't love at all, I saw now — was the second I felt a spark ignite in my heart.

We all know the flame to make love burn needs a spark.

"Let's shower together," I said to Freya.

She gave me a tight, little smile. "I shower alone, my love," she answered.

"But I could soap you all over," I began, licking my lips at the very thought.

She put her finger across my lips to shush me. "No," she said. "A girl has to have her time after the making of the love to gather her own senses."

I shrugged and lay back down, as she pulled herself up. I devoured her body with my eyes, desperate to know every curve, every pimple, every hair. Her skin was so white I could see the red imprints still of where my fingers had dug into her, when my ecstasy had been at its height.

I heard Freya's shower spray into life and got dressed. I poked my head around her bathroom door and shouted, "I'm going upstairs to prepare my paints. Let yourself in."

"Ja, ja," I heard.

I took a boot off at my own front door, to prop it open and kicked the other one off in the direction of my bed.

It was a dull, grey day and no sunlight shone in my large windows to illuminate where Freya would stand. I frowned, looking around my room where I would soon paint the curves of her flesh and the lines that made up her face, eyeing the small pack of white I would need for her voluptuous mane.

I put my radiators on to warm the room and keep her skin warm, and went around lighting some candles.

I caught myself humming.

"Jesus," I muttered, but happily. "A flash of boobs and I'm singing Celine fucking Dion."

I had just set down the last candle on my window sill when I felt arms tickle my ribs and hold me tight across my stomach. Resting my head back, I could smell the cleanliness of Freya, and I sighed contentedly.

"I never heard you sneak in," I said.

"I don't sneak," she replied. "You just listen in other places."

"Get your clothes off," I growled. "Or it won't be listening I am doing to your other places."

She did her gliding twist across my dusty floor, dropping clothes as she turned this way and that, all the while me thinking I might pass out from the lust that was flowing through my veins.

If I don't have this woman, I'll... I'll what? Wait for another ten years, driving myself truly mad? It was not the time for me to get lost in my head and I picked up my brush, as Freya stood posing where she had before.

I pulled the cover off my canvas and began to mix my paints.

"You are beautiful," I said.

"*Vakker*," she told me.

"*Vakker* is beautiful?" I asked. She nodded. "*Vakker*," I repeated.

Then I remembered words spoken before. "*Vakker kjaerlighet*. What does that mean?"

"Beautiful love," she whispered.

I tried to bring up the memory of her saying this, desperately trying to hear her say the words but my mind would not obey and I gave up, knowing I would remember one day because important words always burn somewhere deep down.

I forgot about this, like I try to forget about all unpleasantness when I can, and started to use my brush. I filled my eyes with the beauty of Freya's body and let the flutters of delight it sent through me find their way down my arm to the hand that guided the swipes.

She was going to be my work of art.

Freya stood in front of my windows naked, her hands clasped behind her back, her head turned to her right, gazing away from me. Seeing her filled me with a joy I could not contain, as I realised I was painting furiously with a smile on my face. I took a moment to consider her form, to see where the shadow of her breasts fell on her stomach and I knew then I was falling in love, because love is safer looked at from a distance.

I felt the breath run from my lungs as the shock of this knowledge hit me. I couldn't decide if I was in Heaven or in Hell. Life is always a choice: to break the heart or to heal the heart.

Freya or Helena?

Helena was married, having a child with a man called Edmund.

Freya looked at me with animated eyes full of longing and offered passion.

I unconsciously took a step towards Freya because it was the only thing I could do to protect my fragile heart. Love is the fiercest armour you can wear.

She saw me smiling and asked, "My Nick, I see you are amused by a comedy. You must share this with me."

"I must?" I teased.

"Oh, you must," she insisted, bringing her hands to rest on her hips.

I smiled harder. "You are just fucking perfect," I told her.

"No thing is perfect," she replied.

"You're as near as I'd like to go," I said.

I painted what I could that day before the urges in the tips of my fingers overtook me and I had to touch Freya's body.

I had to. This was no longer a choice. There was a pull to her that I felt each time our eyes met that closed the distance between us and created a heart with chambers of eight, not four.

If she ran, my heart beat faster.

Those moments when I opened my eyes to begin a new day that was mine, I immediately found my thoughts turning to my beloved Freya, who with her ice had cooled the flames that had burned only for Helena. I felt the scales I had put on my eyes, to blind me, had been ripped off and the world I now saw was beautiful and full of light.

"I love you," I panted to Freya, as I thrust on top of her, feeling the slide of her skin over mine and loving the textures of her touches.

"*Jeg elsker deg*," she whispered.

When words are spoken at the moment where your love is riding a wave and the fingers of your lover tweak the veins to your heart, they are embroidered on the soul.

"*Jeg elsker deg*," I repeated.

To a Norwegian, this is more than love and I understood I was the world to Freya. It made me humble, and nice, and all I could think of was ways to please her. I sat with her, asking questions to learn her background, what she liked and hated, to know why plants flourished when she fed them and, most importantly, to see where her passions lay.

Because a heart that cannot be passionate about even a slug if that is its choice, cannot be passionate when it matters most.

She brought a laughter to my face that hurt my cheeks and when she would ask what I laughed at, my stomach would hurt trying to get the words out. She was a joy so delicious I wanted to spend every second with her beside me, because that kept me calm and quietened the voice in my head.

Behind every love is doubt.

I would sneak off to my bed alone at night, waiting for the black of Nikki to overtake me, and even before she arrived, I could hear the mocking taunts.

"Poor. Ugly. Bitter. Lonely. Unloveable."

Nikki made me want to cry. All day I was being kept happy now by Freya, now that I had let her in and still that twisted voice found its way to me.

I would never be free. Not completely. Unless…

I was head over heels in love with Freya and I had never been more afraid in my life. After all, what is love but a delusion? A trick of the mind to bring the veneer of happiness to empty and lacklustre lives.

My life is someone else's.

Now I need it to be mine. That is my only chance at real happiness. I knew instantly what I had to do.

Searching for a card that read 'Mavis Street: Dwarf Adventurer', I rang the number.

"Hello, this is Mavis Street speaking," I heard, remembering the honey drips of her voice.

"Hello, Miss Street. My name is Nick, I'm a friend of Freya."

"I remember you, Nick. I never forget a face. What can I do for you?"

I cleared my throat because I am not pushy by nature but I had a goal now to strive to. "You mentioned that you'd like to have your portrait painted. I was wondering if you were serious."

"Of course I was. Five thousand," she said, tossing the figure out. I've come to realise that the rich throw money around like buttons while I, the poor, scramble for pennies.

"You'll pay me five grand?" I said in disbelief.

"Is that too little?" she asked.

"No, no," I assured her.

Five thousand pounds was more than enough for what I needed, so we agreed the details. I would paint a portrait of Mavis Street but as she was departing soon for an adventure, she did not have time to pose. I would paint her from photographs I would take at my earliest convenience.

It was a perfect excuse to walk over with Freya, as I had to borrow her camera, and we swang our hands together as we walked through the sunshine streets that would take us to the home of Mavis.

It made my heart thud with happiness to spend simple hours with Freya, whose calm washed over me. I couldn't help but smile when she spoke to me, telling me everyday things, because these were the thoughts from her mind I was honoured she would share with me.

"*Jeg elsker deg*," I whispered, as she chatted on about something or other.

It stopped her, because she always heard my love calling to her. "Every time you say that," she told me, "My heart jumps up in a million pieces and falls back into one."

At Mavis' house, we had a cup of tea while her and Freya caught up on their gossip and I figured out how to use the camera. When I was ready, I took snaps from all angles. I would get them enlarged and printed, to hang on my walls for me to paint from. I'd done this before so I was confident I could do a good job and Mavis had an unusual face: what painter would not delight in this challenge? Beauty is not always a straight line.

On my way home, Freya said, "Who is Helena?"

I felt my legs stutter in their steps before I regained my composure because I hadn't been expecting this. Ethel and her big mouth.

"Helena is a woman I used to love a long, long time ago," I told her, quietly.

"You have no love now for her?"

"I don't know." I wanted to be honest with Freya but I didn't want to hurt her feelings with my indecision. Since I had allowed her in, I had tried not to think of Helena, pushing down any thought of her that struggled to emerge.

"I mean for you to tell me who she is, about her. I need to know your past."

My past. Where was it?

My life was like a figment of someone else's imagination, thrown high into the air to see how it would land. I could conjure from memory a day that might be yesterday or tomorrow. Time didn't always move forward, it was a ball of events that rolled around and sometimes, I came out on top.

Helena, Helena, the ball rolls around to a different moment in my life.

*** *** ***

I have a fizz of excitement sizzling at the bottom of my stomach. For a moment I worry it might be nausea until I realise it is anticipation.

Anticipation that any second now, my Helena is going to come gliding through the classroom door and join me at my table, where we sit together every Friday afternoon for double Maths.

As she arrives, her brown curls bouncing, I watch her as she immediately finds me with her eyes and, seeing me, her face explodes into a smile of delight.

The fizz in my tummy works its way down and I shift in my seat. Already we are lovers at this tender age and I know the joys that she brings me in the warmth of her bed.

She slides in beside me, deliberately scraping her chair closer to mine because every inch apart may as well be a mile. Under the table, her hand slides over my skirt, squeezing my leg.

"Helena!" I hiss under my breath, terrified that we will be seen and taunted.

She laughed, squeezing me again, before seeing to her books.

I took a minute to compose myself, to remember once again that she really did love me and that luck had shone on me to give me a beauty such as her.

Later that night, it was me who saw the other side of Helena, when she held me tight after our hurried love-making in her bedroom at her parents house and buried her face in my breasts.

"Please don't leave me," she sobbed.

"I'll never leave you," I tried to comfort.

"You will," she cried. "And my heart will break."

"Shh, my love. There will never be another you."

When consoled she would kiss me, mixing tears and saliva with lust and gratitude. This was the Helena that no-one saw; where her heart leapt out to join mine and her arms opened to vulnerability; where every defence came down and she was just a lost, little girl in need of tender loving.

I was reminded of how our strengths and weaknesses had complemented each other. Alone, she was the one who needed my assurances but to the world, she was the glue that held me together and gave me the belief to put one foot in front of another.

The day a gang of girls surrounded us in the Physical Education changing rooms, circling us like vultures ready to pick at our bones at the slightest hint of weakness.

The biggest girl squared up to me, as I looked to the floor avoiding eye contact, hoping to divert a confrontation.

Her face was close to mine as she mocked me. "Like a bit of fanny, do ye, Nick?"

"No," I mumbled.

She pushed me and I stumbled back. "You're a fucking lezza."

Helena stood forward, putting her face to the bullies. "And what are you going to do about it, eh?" she said, poking her finger in the girl's chest.

"It's disgusting," the girl said, but I could see her step back, realising perhaps the brunt of Helena's temper was not something she wished to be on the end of.

"Your face is fucking disgusting!" Helena shot back. One of the girls behind the bully had giggled and was thrown a stern look.

I know if it had come to blows, Helena would have taken them on the chin for me. She always put herself between me and harm, knowing I had no stomach for upset.

"I don't care about other people," she would tell me, over and over. "I only care about you."

We would hold each other, letting love fill the quiet and Helena would say beautiful things in my ear. She would tell me how much she loved me and that I was all she ever wanted. I was Tracy to her Hepburn, Burton to her Taylor, Bogart to Bacall. Then, she would talk of her daydreams and hopes for our future: that she wanted to go to University and study architecture, so that she might get a job designing; we would get a little place together and I'd have a room to paint in because she knew my passion, after her, was to create my visions on canvas; she went on that we could get a car, laughing that this is what proper lesbian couples did; but her final dream was to get married and start a family with me.

"Imagine it, Nick. Our own little family. The very thought makes me well up. That I could have you forever and we could bring up a child, that is the stuff that dreams are made of."

"I'll do anything for you," I told her, unwavering in my complete devotion.

But don't be fooled — the devotion went both ways, an unbreakable bond between two elements of love, making our life compound. My obsession was equalled by her own. When I smiled, she smiled and when I kissed her, she kissed me back harder. She made an hour with her pass in a second and a night without her became as though a year. All I ever longed for was her to be beside me, to lead our way with her bravery and strength, and I would hold her up with the ferocity of my love. Together we would face life.

Until, until...life got in the way.

How had I let this happen? Even thinking about it made me rub my head. I had promised her, I had given her my word, I had taken her heart from her only to desert her when she had needed me most.

I had gone against everything I had said, broken every vow I had made and brought this misery on myself. I should have known better, I should have trusted in her and kept on at her parents to let me see her, instead of scurrying away like a dog that had been kicked, tail between my legs.

What had I done?

I had the dream and I let it slip through my fingers. And she still loved me! I didn't need her to say this to know it. I knew Helena better than I knew myself and she might have moved on but that was for show. Underneath the marriage and terraced house, she was my Helena and my Helena would never be fully tamed.

"Nick, you're crying," I heard Freya say, in a quiet, scared voice and I saw that we had reached our block of flats.

She moved to wipe my teary face with her delicate, white hands — hands that had almost torn me away — and I jolted back, no longer able to welcome her touch.

"I have to be alone," I said, moving quickly past her to get to the stairs up to my flat.

"Nick! What is wrong?" I heard her say but I couldn't answer as I unlocked my door with shaking hands.

I had come so close to loving Freya. Should I? Should I wait for Helena?

I ran to my kitchen and hastily found myself some vodka to steady my nerves.

Thinking of Helena had re-awakened all the love we had once shared, that had been numbed in me over time. Now that fire was truly burning and the only thing to dampen it was the ice of Freya.

I rubbed my head, cursing Nikki. It was all her fault. She got the good life and I got the misery and heartbreak and indecision, with any chance of happiness always snatched away so that all joy and delight was hers.

I threw my glass the length of the room, shattering it into pieces and grabbed the bottle to drink straight from the neck.

I found my phone and dialled a familiar number.

"Hello, George Chan speaking."

"Mr Chan, it's Nick."

"Oh," he said, with a hint of annoyance in his voice. "No Jackie now, eh? What you want?"

"I want you to find someone for me."

"I want money first."

"I've got the money," I told him, knowing I could borrow off Ethel on the back of the commission from Mavis Street.

"Oh, okay," he softened, annoyance overtaken by greed. "Who you want me find?"

"Her name is Nikki."

CHAPTER NINE

My eyes jolted open as I sucked in a desperate breath. She was going to send someone to find me? To what end? Annoyed and irritated, I swung out of bed and stomped to the bathroom. Well, bring it on. Maybe this was a good thing, to finally meet each other and see what the hell was connecting us. And if she wanted to use her first decent payment to find me rather than better her life, that was her prerogative.

Funny, a week or two ago this would have consumed my thoughts as I tried to work out her reasoning and motives, but today I needed to focus on more important issues.

The Indian lady.

I needed to talk to someone about this and I remembered how supportive Amanda had been when I'd told her about Poppy – maybe she'd be able to help straighten my head out with this? What other option did I have?

I spent half an hour making sure I was suitably presentable (and also sex-ready, just in case…) then headed across the road… *street*, goddammit. I had to sort this leaky Brit-shit out!

Forgetting my manners and annoyed at myself, I banged on the door several times, chewing on my fingernail while I waited for someone to let me in. I was both surprised and suddenly nervous when I saw Ness.

"Oh, er…hey. How's it going?"

"Mom's not here." She went to shut the door, but I put my hand out to stop her.

"Wait, please. I just need to talk to someone, please? Will you talk to me?"

"I'm not very good at advice…"

"I don't care, I just have to get this off my chest before it drives me crazy. Please?" I begged, suddenly desperate for her company. She studied me for a while, frowning.

"I have rehearsal in an hour. If you give me a ride there then I'll hear you out," she said quietly. I felt a surge of something I couldn't quite put my finger on. Was I crushing on Ness now? Jeez, my loins were all over the place lately.

"Done deal. But…can we go to my studio? I don't want us to be overheard."

She agreed and shut the front door behind her before following me silently back to my place.

Once inside my studio I sat on the edge of my spare bed and, to my complete and utter surprise, started right at the beginning. Yes, I told her *everything*. From Nick and our shared time shifts, to my recent experience in the desert and the strange words spoken by the Indian lady.

Ness didn't say a word the whole time. She didn't ask any questions, she didn't express surprise or shock or even mock me — her face remained completely neutral. When I'd finished I just rubbed my face and waited for the laughter.

"You probably think I'm crazy, right?"

"Are you?"

"I don't know. Genuinely. Maybe I am? What do you think?"

"I don't know, Nikki. You said you didn't want my advice, but I don't understand what you *do* want from me?"

I stared at the window, to the flawless deep azure sky beyond the pane. "Something normal. I want something normal in my life. I think I need an anchor to remind me not to float away with it all."

There was a long silence and my god, if all my energy wasn't just slipping away from me right now. I was tired of my life, tired of sharing it with *Her*. I felt tears slide down my cheeks, a journey of release from finally telling my story to someone. Someone real. Ness came and sat next to me, shyly taking my hand.

"I can only offer you my friendship."

"That's enough! That's all I need," I whispered, clutching at it gratefully with my clammy palm.

I got Ness to her rehearsal about fifteen minutes late and stayed to watch. Once again I was mesmerised by her beauty and grace on the ice — if I created art, then she was living, fluid, breathing art. I'm not sure I breathed the whole time she danced, and 'danced' was such a loose term for what she did! She was one with the music which seemed to flow for her, not the other way round. The music worshipped her movements and shaped itself around her.

My paintings were a steaming pile of dog shit next to Ness on the ice.

When she'd finished and came to meet me outside in the parking lot, I was unable to look her in the eye and my mouth could form no words for fear of mumbling nonsense. She stared at me awkwardly.

"What is it? Is something wrong?"

How could I articulate my feelings without scaring her away from me for good? I shook my head and attempted a weak smile.

"No. Let's go."

There was something reassuring in her arms holding me as we rode home and I felt a calm cloud settle around me. I also felt a surge of something else, an urgency I recognised would need to be addressed straight away. As soon as we'd said our goodbyes, I ran to my workshop and locked the door behind me. Within minutes I'd hung the largest piece of plain canvas I had from the ceiling and, as if in a trance, started to paint.

*** *** ***

It was five days before I emerged from my creative hole and when I did, I was chilled to the bone with what I saw. After staring at it for more than an hour, I called Ness and asked her if she could come over immediately — she did, to my relief, and I showed her my newest painting.

"Nikki…what is this?" she asked, frowning up at it.

"Not my best, that's for sure."

There was a long pause.

"I'm sorry, I just don't like it."

"That makes two of us."

The picture loomed ominously down at us, a dark portrayal of anger and pain and torment. The twisted figure of a girl sat sideways against a wall, hugging her chest with her legs askew as she stared blankly into space. Standing above and behind her a tall dark female screaming with such an intense fury it made all the hairs on my body stand erect, as if the roots wanted to escape the bindings of my skin and flee.

"Nikki?"

"Mm?"

"Were they meant to look like you?"

"I think so. I think the one on the floor is me, and the other one is Nick. It's almost like…she looks like the shadow of the one on the floor, right?"

Ness tilted her head and moved reluctantly forward to inspect it.

"Yeah, I can see that."

"I think it kinda represents that Nick is the darker version of me…and that she wants to hurt me," I whispered, hugging my arms to my chest as if copying the picture version of me.

Before we could say anything else, there was a loud banging on the door, making us both jump. Knowing mom would never bang the door in such a manner, and feeling irrationally that it might be Nick, I turned the canvas around to face the wall and told Ness to stay put. Heart in my mouth I stumbled to the door and peered nervously out, the trepidation turning to irritation. I opened it enough to talk through the gap.

"Malena, what the hell is your problem?"

To my surprise she pushed her way into my studio, forcing me to step back off balance before I could chase after her.

"Where is she? Are you fucking her already?"

"What? It's none of your business!"

I managed to catch her just as she reached Ness and the painting. Her sixth sense must have cottoned on to the hidden canvas because she seemed to aim straight for it.

"What's this? A new portrait?" she sneered as she tried to turn it around and a dark fury flooded my veins. How DARE she! I grabbed her arm and swung her round to face me while simultaneously drawing back my free hand ready to slap her...but it was stopped in mid-air. Ness was holding it in her own cool hand, her eyes calming my temper like sand on flames as she addressed Malena.

"I don't know who you are, and if I'm honest, I don't care too much either, but Nikki and I aren't anything more than just good friends so how about I just leave you both to chat things over?" she said, releasing my arm and casually moving towards the exit. I didn't want her to leave, I wanted Malena to go. My guilt over the death of Poppy was not so strong and obliging now.

"That's a great idea. Fuck off," Malena growled, not seeming to care for any other female, friend or otherwise, in my company.

I seethed, opening my mouth to tell her to get out instead but Ness got my attention, smiled at me and said, "I'll catch up with you tomorrow. I have rehearsal at three, 'kay?"

When I nodded, she gave a quick nod back then left. I knew she meant for me to take her to her practice and that she was aware my current situation needed to be dealt with.

"What the hell is wrong with you? How dare you come barging on into my studio like this?" I said, my voice loud enough to convey how pissed I was, but also with warning that I was on the verge of losing my shit at any second. She stared at me, a muscle working in her jaw.

"Are you fucking her?"

"It's none of your goddamn business if I am, I'm a free agent!"

"Maybe someone should warn her, let her know what you're like, huh? Tell her how you just take what you want then lose interest when you've had enough? I thought you were nice but I'm glad Poppy didn't have to go through this!"

I stared at Malena in shock. Her outburst had hit all the right spots and shame flooded me as I tried to avoid her blazing eyes.

"You're right. I'm sorry. Oh god, I'm so sorry," I muttered, my shoulders sagging as I walked over to the couch and sat on it, feeling surprisingly tired. I expected her to leave, or shout some more to take advantage of my vulnerable state, but she came and sat next to me.

"Why? Why do you behave like this Nikki? Are you hurtin' about Poppy still or have you always been like this?"

I sighed, her compassion hitting me harder than her angry words. "I don't know why I behave like this. I guess I've always been like it, but I don't know why. You're the first person to show me the effect my actions have."

Malena put her arm around my shoulders and hugged me.

"Maybe it's time to change, huh?"

I nodded, allowing tears to roll down my cheeks as I leaned into her warm embrace, yearning for her soft femininity which felt comforting and safe in that moment.

She stayed for the rest of the day and night. I asked her about Poppy and how they'd grown up together, wanting to know about the girl we'd both had taken from our lives, and Malena had a thousand stories to tell. She laughed and cried through them all, then confessed her family were all avoiding any kind of reminder of Poppy and any slight mention of her sister was shushed swiftly. I encouraged more stories out of her and when I knew my day was over, she held me close and stroked my hair soothingly until my eyes shut.

When I reopened them the next morning, she was snuggled into me. I watched her sleep, feeling a certain sense of affection for her. When she finally awoke, before we even said two words to each other, we made love.

*** *** ***

I revved Monster gently while I waited for Ness, feeling confused and excited at the same time. I hadn't felt guilty about sleeping with Malena, but I still wanted Ness.

Didn't I?

I watched as she left the house, jogging across the yard with a small amount of urgency. Before I could even say hi, Amanda came out behind her, looking fresh and friendly, and I suddenly felt nervous. It was too late to make a getaway so I took a deep breath and prepared to say hello and face the music.

"Hey stranger, where you been?"

"I had an, er, important piece I needed to finish. Sorry."

Amanda looked from Ness to me and back at her daughter, curiously amused.

"There something I should know?"

"No!" Ness said, looking appalled at the idea. I swallowed and forced a laugh.

"We're just hanging out is all. I'm giving her a ride to the rink."

Ness shuffled uncomfortably, I cleared my throat and Amanda narrowed her eyes.

"Sure. Well, be sure to pop in and see me soon, or I can come over to your place and we could have a bit more privacy…whatever suits you."

I nodded emphatically, certain she could tell I had no intention of doing either.

"Definitely. Soooo anyway, we'd better hit the road, Ness. You ready?"

She nodded and got on behind me, then with a small wave, I tried my best not to wheel spin down the road.

We didn't say much when we got to the arena, but while she put her skates on and warmed up, I tried to locate the best place to view her dance. Then I sat on the edge of the seat and waited.

She didn't disappoint. Her dancing was entrancing — she blinded my imagination with her ownership of the ice, a blank canvas for her moving visual art. I wanted, no, I *craved*, to watch her all night. She was a muse to me, except instead of wanting to create anything, I was content in watching her be the creator of wonder in my mind.

Once again I was rendered mute and useless, feeling like a limp rubber doll when she emerged from the showers and walked shyly up to where I sat.

"Hey, you okay?"

"Ness, you…you hypnotise me."

She sat next to me and sighed.

"Don't. I told you I can't be anything more than your friend."

"I'm not worthy of even being your friend, let alone anything else! My god, you are a Goddess."

"Nikki, please…" She tilted her head back to look up at the ceiling. "I'm not that person. I'm just a normal girl who can skate."

"No, you're not normal by a long shot! The way you express your art…it's exquisite! How long have you been skating? What got you started?"

"You know, the usual way people get into hobbies. I just hit the ice one day and realised how much I enjoyed it." Her answer seemed mechanical, as if it was what she told everyone who asked. I turned to face her.

"Now why don't you tell me the real reason?"

"Aw, c'mon, you don't really wanna know my boring history."

"I one hundred percent do."

"Don't humor me. No one ever wants to know about me," she said quietly. "It starts out that way, but then the questions come. 'So, like, what's the deal with your parents, dude' and 'Do you all just like sleep together in one big fucking orgy, or what?' Or there's my favorite, 'Is it cool if I ask your mom out on a date?'" Ness mimicked, showing her frustration at the ignorant mentality. "People just use me as an angle to get more information on what my family get up to."

"Well, since I already know what your family gets up to, you can just go ahead 'n' trust me. I'm genuinely interested in hearing about you, just you, and no one else but you."

"I just...why? Why are you so interested in me?"

I smiled and took her hand — it was warm and damp against my cold one.

"Because you're interesting, and beautiful and passionate about what you do. I want to know your past as well as be in your present...and then maybe see what happens in the future. Not like that," I added quickly, not wanting to freak her out. "So, c'mon, tell me. Where'd it all begin?"

She took a deep breath and let it out slowly.

"Music. It all began when I started listening to music. As a kid, I felt music right through to the core of my being, and not like all my friends seemed to. They liked all the latest releases, young boy bands et cetera. I listened to classical music, old records from the forties and fifties, jazz, y'know, stuff seven year olds don't normally go for. It was almost a dirty little secret if I'm honest." She shook her head and chuckled. "It feels weird telling you this. I haven't told anyone this before."

"Ness, I recently told you I share consciousness with a girl who lives in Scotland...I think I out-trump you in weird confessions!"

She laughed — I think it was the first time I'd heard her laugh so freely and it made me feel warm throughout despite the icy environment. I decided I wanted to make her laugh more.

"I'm still not sure you aren't just crazy."

"Maybe I am. But we're talking about you right now, not me. When did this love of music develop into skating?"

Ness hesitated slightly, and I could see she was genuinely touched by my interest in her art.

"Well, I used to dance to the music in my room, desperately trying to express it as much as I could. It was like an itch that needed scratching, but intensely frustrating cos I couldn't seem to scratch it by dancing...it just kinda tickled it more. It was too confined, too restricted.

One day, when I was about nine years old, I was leaping around with my headphones on and I misjudged the height of the wall I was jumping off, tryna copy Kevin Bacon in *Footloose!*" She smiled a secret smile. "I've never told anyone that before."

"Your secret's safe with me." I made a zipping motion across my mouth.

"So anyway, I landed wrong on my foot and twisted it. It wasn't a bad injury, just a sprain, but it meant I was unable to dance for a couple of weeks and that made me more frustrated and really angry." She looked at me. "Do you believe in destiny Nikki?"

I nodded.

"During those two weeks I was laid up on the sofa, ordering mom to bring me chips and hot chocolate while I zoned out at the box. I was in such a big sulk, I refused to listen to any music — if I couldn't dance to it, I wasn't gonna listen to it. But on the third day, the winter Olympics started and I became hooked on it, on the ice dancing in particular. I mean, these guys were dancing to all kinds of music...and I remember watching them and feeling a huge clarity settle over me. This was it! This was the answer I'd been searching for the whole time. The way they moved across the ice, the jumps, the spins...you could see the pure emotion on their faces because they weren't just dancing to the music, they were *feeling* it in their souls!"

Every hair on my arms stood to attention. I could practically see nine year old Ness sat on the sofa, engrossed in the wonder of the winter Olympics.

"And I knew then…that was what I was going to do, no matter what. As soon as my ankle healed I went to the nearest rink, hired some skates and taught myself to move on the ice."

"How long did it take to learn how to dance?"

"Couple of years, to get to a level where I was satisfied with expressing myself. Mom put me into a few competitions, and I guess I only went along with it in the beginning cos I got to have the ice to myself when I trained, and it felt so good not to have to share the space with anyone. But I enjoy the training more than the competing. God, I *hate* the competing."

We sat in silence for a minute.

"Shame. Cos you're good enough to compete at Olympic level."

"No, uh-uh. I wouldn't want to start feeling like I'm constantly in competition. Like people would always be judging my moves, whether or not I'm good enough, pushing me to be better and work harder. I skate for myself, for my enjoyment. It gets technical and detached in competitions, worrying about where I'm gonna place and if I'm gonna lose my sponsorship. I'm happy where I am."

My cell buzzed in my pocket and I pulled it out with a small apology.

"It's mom. She wants me to pick up some books from the library."

"On your bike?"

"I have a back-pack at home. It's big enough for small supplies," I explained, feeling a small amount of regret that our chat had ended but also guilt that I'd neglected my mother lately.

"I've really enjoyed talking to you today."

"Me too."

I felt that spinning in my stomach, the excited kind of spinning when you know you're at the beginning of something beautiful with someone.

Yep, Ness and I were going to be good, good friends.

CHAPTER TEN

I'm swimming in a sea of fire, burning my arms as I struggle against the tide that tries to pull me under. In the distance, I see an iceberg, somehow remaining solid in the surrounds of this heat. I swim harder, trying to reach it because I know somehow that I will be safe if I can reach there, I'll be grounded.

My head swims in fire and ice.

Freya's face swoops before me, bringing a damp cloth to my brow and I close my eyes again, too weak to fight the call of the dark.

Somewhere, in the back of my deranged mind, I realise I am unwell and am fighting fevers and infection. One minute the sweats overtake me, the next I am shivering with the cold. First it is Helena's face swimming before me, then it is Freya's.

The hot and the cold.

There are dabs on my lips, monsters oozing from the cracks in my walls, covers being pulled up to my chin, raised voices, screams and shouts.

And in the midst of this madness, there is always the face of Nikki. Her evil sneer is dancing in front of my eyes as she pours forth the venom to belittle me. Seeing her though gives me the will to fight because I will not let her win. I haven't loved for nothing and I *will* love again. I will not have her suck the joy from my life with her quiet taunts. She might be on the other side of the world but she seems a whisker away every second, almost like my next breath could be hers. There is nothing separating us but hatred.

It's been this way for as long as I can remember. Whatever I did, Nikki did it better. If I painted a picture, Nikki sold one of hers for a fortune. I had the love of one woman and Nikki had her pick of the bunch. I scraped through school and she aced her exams with barely an hour of study. Everything she turned her hand to succeeded, while I lived in poverty and despair.

Every piece of luck I could ever have had and she had to snatch it away for herself like a petulant child. Every bad decision I made was because of her, I could see this now and it was her jealousy that was keeping me from finding love.

My fever raged on for days but the voices became still.

*** *** ***

When I awoke feeling better, the first thing I heard was the silence. The stillness of my mind had infiltrated my flat and numbed all noise.

I sat up in bed on my elbows and flexed my jaw to pop my ears. I looked around my flat which was exactly as it always was and yet... yet, something had changed.

I heard my stomach rumble, relieved I was no longer deaf, and got out of bed to find some clothes before I made myself something to eat.

I had no idea how long I had been ill for. It could have been hours, it could have been days. Time never ran in a straight line when I was being dragged between Heaven and Hell.

Opening my fridge, I saw with surprise and delight that it was full. Ethel must have stocked up for me while I was unconscious. My hungry eyes were grateful and I grabbed some ham and cheese to make a sandwich. The ham was a children's pack called 'Billy Bear', slices of ham shaped into the face of a bear. I had practically lived on it through my teens. Helena used to buy it in special for me.

Helena.

Could she have been here and done this for me? I looked around and saw a sleeve of cigarettes next to the microwave, with my Zippo lighter atop. The lighter that she had given me.

I smiled because I had known she still loved me and I was right. I felt my heart soar and a grin began at the corners of my mouth. She had come back to reclaim her lost love.

I ate my sandwich, my eyes landing on my covered canvas and I was reminded that not only had I to finish the one I started of Freya but I had her dwarf pal's commission.

I was still hungry though and found a new packet of 'Frosties' in the cupboard. Another old favourite of mine. Helena and I used to watch videos in her bedroom and I would always have my hand stuck in a box of 'Frosties'. Who needed milk?

The little things always make me happy. I am so used to being miserable that any excuse for happiness, however small, will suffice.

I heard my phone ring and hurried to answer, my hopes momentarily raised but it was only Ethel.

"Are you feeling better, sweetness?" she asked.

"Yes, thanks. Did you stock my fridge?"

"Oh no, that wasn't me," she told me.

"Do you know who it was?" I had to know.

"You caused quite a ruckus while you were away with the fairies."

"What do you mean?" I asked, suspiciously.

"It's not my place to say…" she trailed off, knowing I would be eager to find out.

"Spit it out, mother."

"Let me put it this way, you were the object of a little tug of war."

She had to mean Freya and Helena, but before I could press her for further details, she declared there was someone at her door and hung up wishing me well.

So, Freya and Helena *had* been here when I was fevered and, by the sounds of it, had rubbed each other up the wrong way. This was only to be expected as Helena could easily be taken offence at if you didn't know her vulnerability that she kept so well hidden.

I decided to paint and let the day bring to me what it would. I looked at the canvas I had started of naked Freya and a shiver ran through me. There was no denying she was beautiful. But her beauty was almost too much for me to bear and I threw a sheet over her to safeguard my senses.

I began work on the dwarf, content knowing I could live happily for months on the money it would bring in. And then I remembered that I had phoned Mr Chan, the private investigator who had found Helena for me, to find Nikki.

Ah well, he was more likely to find a needle in a haystack. I'd let him look for a bit, just to have some fun with him, then tell him to forget it. The money would be worth paying for his wasted time. If he had found Helena sooner, maybe some heartbreak could have been avoided.

I was losing myself in thoughts when I should have been losing myself in my work and I chastised myself. Paint now, daydream later.

And that's how the next few hours went, my wrist ached and my shoulders screamed from holding my positions with dedication to my art. I looked from photograph to canvas and created an image of Mavis Street that she would surely fall in love with.

Falling in love is the only feeling in the world that matters. At least that's what you think until you realise that the only thing that matters is to feel.

And I *was* feeling. I had love coursing through me, from the smile on my lips to the stroke of my brush, every fibre felt alive, renewed by a hope of Helena.

Happiness had snuck up on me, quietly, like a snake in the grass.

And it wasn't the only thing to have snuck up on me, as I spun around, hearing a creak from my floorboards.

"Helena!"

She had let herself into my flat, probably well aware my door was never locked, and was unbuttoning the expensive looking red woollen coat that danced to her knees.

I was mesmerised, watching how expertly her fingers found the buttons and moved deftly to twist them through the holes. In days gone by, I had been undone by those same fingers and I couldn't help but feel a tremble inside, knowing I would be undone again.

"You're out of bed, Nick. Are you feeling better? You had me worried for a time," she said, speaking softly with confidence, as she slid her coat off her arms, folding it neatly on my bed.

"Yes, I'm much better, thanks. But what are you doing here?" I asked, hoping I wasn't still fevered.

"I'm here to look after you. I've been here every day wiping your forehead and moistening your cracked lips. Don't you remember anything of the last few days?"

"No," I told her. "Just the fever nightmares."

"I'll make us tea," she said, heading towards the kettle.

"Helena, that doesn't answer why you're here. The last time I saw you... well, you didn't exactly fill me with hope for us."

"I told you I'd call," she said, getting two cups ready for tea. "And I did call. Your mother answered your phone and told me you were ill, so I came over and when I saw you lying there so helpless, I knew I couldn't go back to a life without you in it."

"Hang on," I said, puzzled by what I was hearing simply because it was too good to be true. "Are you telling me that you want us to get back together?"

"Sit down and have some tea," I was told and having no choice, I put down my brush and went to my sofa where she had made herself comfortable.

I lifted the warm cup and drank too greedily, burning my lips. "Ow!" I complained.

She turned me to her and ran her finger along my lips. My stomach lurched with old desires as my eyes held the darkness of hers. She smiled over her shoulder as she made her way back to the kitchen for her cup.

It took me back in time to our first kiss. A first kiss should never be forgotten. It takes two people and changes how they will look at each other forever.

We were fourteen, best friends, but more than that, unable to pass a day without each other's company. Helena had made every day bearable for me then.

We used to cuddle in her bedroom, watching film after film, and this night, I had decided to wash her feet. I had gotten a basin of hot water, a bar of soap, a flannel and some towels.

She had sat on the edge of her bed, saying nothing, just watching intently as I undid her laces, lifting her leg to ease off her shoes. I slid my hands down her ankles, helping her socks off and brought her feet down into the warm water. I had smiled then because she had wiggled her toes.

Taking my time, I had wet the flannel, soaped it and began to wash her foot. I put every inch of myself into that cleansing, making sure no part was missed. When they were both clean, I lifted them onto a towel placed on the floor and dried them with the second towel.

I remember the pulse throbbing at the side of my head and I knew she was the only thing that could make it better.

I stood up and pushed her back on her shoulders so that she reclined on her bed. Then I lay on top of her and nuzzled into her neck. I felt the thrust of her hips against mine as her arms went around me, pulling me in. I let myself be taken over by my teenage lust and thrust my hips back into her, nestling our legs into the optimum position for grinding, even before we knew what that was.

"Oh, God," I moaned. "If we don't stop this, I'll end up kissing you."

"Kiss me, Nick," she breathed and I needed no second invitation. There was no hesitation as my lips found hers, soft meeting soft, daggers of delight piercing me as her tongue wrapped around mine. All I could do was kiss her. When you kiss someone you are falling in love with, you fall into their kiss and their taste and their softness.

I couldn't breathe but I couldn't tear my lips away. I wanted to melt into her and could have sworn I was with the heat between us.

My eyes were closed and my mind was on her mouth but my love was touching another part of her.

I opened my eyes and she was staring up at me, her lips still juicy. For a second, panic rose that she was horrified, that her stare was one of anger and I would shortly be heaved off her and thrown out, never to darken her door again or to mention this indiscretion.

But I needn't have worried. Helena never let me down. Whenever I doubted her, she invariably proved me wrong.

Her eyes welled with tears and her bottom lip began to tremble, and just like that panic became fear.

Every emotion is separated by the smallest of degrees. From love to panic to fear in the blink of an eye. The gamut of my heart.

"What's wrong, Helena?" I whispered.

"You love me," she wept.

"Yes," I agreed. "I do love you."

"I was terrified you'd think me a freak," she said, continuing to cry.

I put my finger to her cheek to wipe her tears, smoothing them out across her baby soft skin. "You're no more a freak than I am. Are we freaks because we have hearts full of love?"

"Oh, Nick," she sighed, sniffing. "You are such a romantic. Not everyone will see us as pure."

"Then fuck them," I declared, young and full of bolshie spirit.

The smile she gave me burned away my fear and the kiss that followed seared into my soul. Finally we melted together.

That moment seems like yesterday. Every happy memory feels like yesterday. But the misery is a minute ago, breathing down my neck, ready to pounce and remind. And any reminder of misery will beat away a happy memory.

"Nick?" she said, her voice a far away whisper that found me and brought me back to reality.

"Yes, *min kjaerlighet*?" I asked, another person from another time.

"Drink your tea," she commanded and I brought the cup that was before me back to my lips that would welcome any form of kindness.

I watched her, watching me, over the rim of my cup as I drank in the sugary sweetness she had made for me. A cup of tea is oftentimes a cup of love. My fingers warmed and I felt my heart thaw a bit, or a beat. I was no longer able to tell the difference.

"Do you love me, Nick?" she asked.

"Yes," I told her without hesitation because I did. I had always loved her. And I always would. I could have multiple love affairs that would take me from my twenties to my eighties, and still the only love that would make a dent on my life would be the first love that dented my life. Every love that comes after that seems a watered down version, except... except what if I was wrong?

"I love you, Nick," Helena said and I knew then I couldn't possibly be wrong. Love doesn't deceive.

I sneered, unable to help myself because my pain always reared its ugly face as anger. "Oh, now you love me? Now that you are married and up the duff? Are you sure? This room is the sum total of my life: fuck all. I have nothing to give you," I told her.

She marched towards me and I quickly set the cup on the table, thinking she meant to strike me.

"You broke my fucking heart," she wailed, falling to her knees in front of me.

This was not the Helena who stood in her front room surrounded by photos of her and her husband, confident in the security of her life. This was the Helena who had clung to me as a teenager weeping with the fear that I might leave her.

Why *had* I left it so long to find her? Why had my fear trapped me for so long? I could only blame it on my wild heart.

I threw my arms around her, feeling sixteen once more and who doesn't want to be sixteen again, caught up in the trials of their heart that was the only thing that mattered in life? When I first loved Helena, I never knew what it meant to panic over paying my rent, my only concern was that when I woke up the next day she would still love me.

I felt her arms go around my legs as she knelt weeping, her head pushing between my knees as I stooped to keep her near.

This was what I had wanted for the last ten years. I had dreamed of Helena walking back into my life and declaring her undying love. Somehow it felt too good to be to true but here she was, crying on her knees, bent and broken as a small part of me wished on her the misery I'd felt all these years. That, of course, brought the guilt that I could wish pain on the woman I claimed to love.

I immediately felt the remorse as my fingers itched onto her deeper. "I'm sorry," I whispered. "I'm sorry."

"Sorry's not enough," she cried.

"What more can I do?" I wept. "I told you I'd always wait. I came and found you years later and I wasn't the one who had disappeared into another life. *I* waited."

Helena took her arms away from my legs, wiping her eyes, her dark, dark eyes that glared terrors from the night should I dare to look too closely. But still I swam in them unable to fend off my fears because when her eyes met mine, I felt alive and I needed that after feeling dead for years.

"You left me!" she shouted, standing to slap me. I saw her arm reach back, as her face screamed its agony and I saw the hand soar through the space between us until its sharp whip met my cheek. I flinched but I remained. I deserved this.

"If I had known," I began, my cheek smarting. "I would have camped in your garden. I would have smashed your bedroom window with rocks, I would have built a ladder to climb to you. Don't you see?" I beseeched, my hands grabbing hers in mine, forcing her to face me.

She wasn't the only one who had eyes to drown in.

"I was so scared," I carried on, seeing I had her attention. Eyes met eyes and heart met heart as I felt my breath begin in my chest. "I was nothing. I *am* nothing. You had everything: the big house, the lovely parents, the money, the charm. How could I compete? I was all your insecurities and mine rolled into a huge snowball that grew larger the longer we were together. When your mum told me you didn't want me, I believed her!" I shouted. "I knew one day you'd leave me."

Helena wiped a final tear from her eye before it could spill over onto her face. "I waited for you, Nick. And then I waited some more. I guess it's me then that has to say sorry. I believed them, my mum and dad, when they told me that you hadn't come round or contacted them. I was ill but I begged them to tell you and begged them to let you in to see me. They told me they had, you weren't interested, you'd found another girl and I should concentrate on getting well. Life would seem better when I got over my illness."

I hung my head in shame. I had not fought for my love when she had needed me most. How dare I declare a love when I couldn't believe in it. I felt the soft caress of Helena on my shoulder.

"It wasn't your fault," she sighed. "We were young and didn't know any better. We couldn't know fear and prejudice. We had our love but we were frightened by the enormity of it. I wish I had tried harder," she said and I heard the break in her voice as her emotions got the better of her.

That was all it took for me to be lost in Helena once again. That tiny crack in her voice, the sound of love making its way from her heart to her vocal chords, the emotions that I thought

I'd forgotten but it seemed like yesterday I'd heard that same crack when she first declared her love for me.

Sometimes I cracked and heard Nikki.

"I should've tried harder, not you," I mumbled.

"Nick," she breathed into my ear, for we now stood against each other, our bodies touching, my arms itching to reach out and hold her close. "Try now."

I needed no encouragement. I raised my head to see her eyes, to make sure I wasn't dreaming and then I threw myself forward in a great gust to kiss her, to hold her, to feel her against me. I wanted time to move quickly, I wanted Helena to be naked and beneath me. I wanted her head to jolt back in an ecstasy I had provided, her eyes closed and her fists clenched.

That happened but I saw her body was different. There was a bump in her stomach, a child growing from the seed of a man. I ran my hands over it as her eyes searched me fearfully.

"I'll love you both," I said determinedly. "Any part of you is a part of me."

She jolted up and held me, kissing my shoulder. This was the moment I had waited for from a lifetime ago. I'd reached my peak and so had she, as we clung to each other, the ashes of our teenage love burning between us.

I saw her pain, her naked pain and I took it in to myself. Naked Helena, the goosebumps of her legs making stories on mine that I might read later, that I would never forget but I think I've said that before.

"We have to make a plan," she said, pulling her skin from mine so that I could no longer feel her.

"A plan for what?" I asked, propping myself up on my elbows. "Just leave Jiminy Cricket and move in with me. I'll get a job, I'll support us."

Helena said nothing as she got up and started to dress. I got up to throw on my pants and t-shirt, watching her.

"Helena," I said, stopping her with the touch of my palm on her shoulder. "Babe, love me."

Nikki.

"I can't just leave my husband, Nick," she said.

"But, but you love me…" I stammered.

"I do love you, Nick. I fucking love you so much but I can't bring my child up to live in a freezing attic. You can barely support yourself. Look at you. You pretend to be a painter but your mother pays all your bills. You're a bum, baby. I love you and I'll come to you as often as you'll have me, that we can plan, but I'm not going to live in squalor for the sake of love."

I *was* wrong. Love *always* deceives.

I felt my heart fall to my feet.

For a few minutes there love had held it up and now it was down again in the gutter where my passion belonged. How could my love for her bring me such highs and such lows? Was that the nature of love that one minute you're so elated and the next it feels like your life is over and not worth living?

"So, I'm just a fuck?"

She came over to me, her dark eyes gleaming from sex and she kissed me. "No. You'll always be more than that. You're everything to me. I love you. I will always love you. But I'm a snob," she shrugged. "I want the good life. So as much as I can't live without you, I won't live with you like this. And I know you'll be here, you've waited this long," she smiled.

She was back to being cock-sure, arrogant in her power over me and as much as I wanted to drag my heart up from the gutter in which it dwelt, I could do nothing against her.

She was Helena. She was the spark in my soul that ignited my passion. I was the slave to our love.

"You'll wait," she smiled, taking my pathetic face in her hands. "Because you always have. And maybe now you'll find a way."

I watched her go. I'm good at watching the women I love walk away. Like a twig floating down the river, I see them all drift away, further and further from my flexing fingertips that try to grab, as useless as my beating heart.

Helena stood at my door and she turned just to make sure I was looking. Her vulnerability depleted with the security of my love. I gave her what she needed to be strong again and in return I got nothing.

Ingenting.

That made me remember the soft Norwegian words that told me what *'ingenting'* meant.

When you think of love you think of the burning fires of passion. But what when love deceives and all we can surely be left with is the ice of hard desire?

I knew where ice and desire lived.

I had that moment, that tiny instant in time where Helena was back in my arms and the world — the world that was mine for only the briefest of moments — came alive and I danced in the flames of love. I felt fourteen, in love, where no-one could touch me. Not even Nikki.

Not even Nikki.

It was funny how every happy moment in my life ended with a vision of her twisted, jealous face. She was so used to having all the happiness, all the attention, all the glory, that any snippet that fell my way would have to be crushed under her designer shoe.

I was fed up lying down for people to walk all over me. It has been the story of my life and I'm fed up with that fucking slut writing my story for me. It's time I took a hand in my own destiny.

Helena won't be with me, not how I want her to be, until I can give her a grand house, a big car, and a wad of money to spend on maternity dresses. I could do that for her if I didn't have someone's heel pressing my face into the mud to keep me down.

My pain and heartache have simplified my life.

To have Helena, knowing now that she loved me, I'd need to get rid of what held me back.

I punched a number into my mobile, drumming my fingers impatiently as it rang.

"George Chan speaking. How I help you?"

"Mr Chan, it's Nick. Have you found her?"

CHAPTER ELEVEN

I spent the whole day in a daze. She had my address. Nick had my actual address. I wasn't too sure how to process this information and had been unable to get hold of anyone. (Except mom and I obviously wasn't about to divulge this sort of shit to her.)

By the time I was preparing for bed, I got a sudden rush of messages from Malena and Ness - Malena was going to come over when she finished work the next day and Ness had been at some kind of sponsorship meeting before the scout came to watch her skate. I gave her a quick call to see if she was free in the morning for breakfast and we arranged to meet first thing. Then my eyes slammed shut and I was gone.

"What does that mean? That she's coming over to see you?" Ness asked as I filled her in over waffles and coffee.

"She's trying to. She tried to buy a flight yesterday but she forgot about applying for an *esta* so I guess as long as it takes for that to go through? Hey, on the plus side, it's not like she can sneak up on me!"

"I just don't understand how it works? I mean, there isn't even twelve hours difference between the UK and us so why isn't there an overlap? What's gonna happen when you come face to face with each other? Will it be like in *Back To The Future* - y'know, when he says not to meet his older or younger self cos it'll mess the time continuum or something?"

I raised my eyebrow at Ness.

"I have absolutely no idea."

"Hmm," she added, frowning, "She can't sneak up on you, but you also can't hide. She'll always know where you are."

"Thank you. You're really helping me to relax about all this!" I shovelled a large mouthful of waffle into my mouth and scowled at my plate as I chewed.

"Nikki? Don'cha just wanna know? I mean, if she really is coming, maybe you'll both get some answers? Maybe this is a good thing?" Ness offered.

"I've thought about that. I've thought about it a lot, but whenever I think about us meeting...I just get a horrible sinking feeling. Nothing good can come from us making contact. She's not coming over for us to tearfully unite and get to know each other in person, she's coming over to..."

"To what?"

I shrugged.

"To take over my life. To remove me from hers permanently. She wants my money and my identity for herself."

There. I'd said it out loud. It was simple and stupid and totally irrational, but I knew it was her intention. Ness and I sat in silence as we picked at the remnants on our plates.

"What're you gonna do?"

"Not much I can do. She's made her decision and now we're both gonna just have to face each other and see what happens. I looked up how long *Estas* take to get approved — she could be here within the week."

"Isn't there anything we can do? Can't we alert the authorities or, or, what about if I lock you in a room and disappear with the key until you wake up?"

"I already considered something along those lines but how long do we want to be doing that for? It's like she thinks by taking MY life and MY money, this loser Helena is going to suddenly want to be with her. In my opinion, if you love someone you love them. End of. You'd give up everything and go through anything for them." I threw my hands up in exasperation. "On the other hand, I can totally sympathise with this pregnant woman because let's face it, Nick is a bit of a dead end."

"I've never been in love, but I imagine if I was that I'd give up my life for them," Ness said quietly, pushing her plate away. I watched her for a minute but her expression was closed and totally unreadable.

"Has anyone ever said they're in love with you?"

She shook her head but seemed to withdraw further into herself at the question. I debated pushing for the cause of her discomfort but could tell it would only make her pull away more so I tactfully changed the subject and asked about her upcoming meeting with the talent scout. She shrugged.

"I don't know. I mean, obviously it'd be mind blowing if she thought I was good enough for Nationals, but I don't wanna get my hopes up or anything. You know I skate for my own enjoyment — the idea of doing it to please others and then, y'know, disappointing them cos I didn't match up to their expectations or I wasn't as good as my opponents..."

"You're ten times better than any of the skaters I've seen on the box *because* of those reasons Ness. You skate for yourself and you skate from your soul — they're all gunning to be the best and to win and that desperation is what kills their passion."

"But...what if I lose that? What if I get caught up in it all?" Ness asked quietly. It was then, in that gentle flicker of her eyes, that I sensed just how vulnerable she felt about it. This wasn't just a possible career advancement — she was fully aware of what was at stake as this could make or break her love of the sport. I touched her arm and waited for her to look at me.

"I don't think you would but if you did? Well, just quit professional league and go back to small time competitions to keep your sponsors happy!"

"Yeah, I guess that is an option. Oh, by the way, I meant to tell you, mom has her sights set on someone else so you are off the hook," she said, casually ping-ponging the conversation away from herself, as uncomfortable in the spotlight as me it seemed. "Some mechanic she met at a bar a couple of nights ago. He took her out and she didn't get back in 'til this morning, so I hope you don't suddenly change your mind cos she's likely to brush you off."

I sighed with relief — that was one less worry on my mind (although the fact I viewed a hot lady chasing me as a worry was in itself a worry.)

"How's things with Malena?" Ness continued, signalling for more coffee from a passing server.

"Tricky. I feel very confused. In fact...I don't know who's more confused. She isn't gay, and I never go for straight girls. We're both in like a weird shuffle of not knowing what to do with each other!" I laughed and shook my head at the absurdity of the situation. I was sitting opposite a girl I was getting obsessed with, relieved that her hot mom had stopped chasing me, and telling her about my relationship with a dead, potential ex-girlfriend's straight sister! Ness smiled at me, an odd expression in her eyes that I couldn't read but that caused a burst of something into my bloodstream. As it streamed round my veins I struggled to find my voice again, eager to keep the mood light and easy and not scare her off. I cleared my throat. "I don't know. I might not have to even worry about it soon, not if crazy psycho bitch gets here first."

"Hey, if anything happens to you, she won't get away with it. I'll make sure of that, 'k? I've totally got your back." Her cell buzzed and she read the text, frowning. "I've gotta go. Mom wants me to go and make sure the tech at the rink has everything set up ready for Thursday."

"I'll see you tomorrow, right?"

"Sure. I'll be rehearsing all day though."

"I'll take you to the rink and back on the bike if you want? Save you from Mika in the car," I said, referring to the cd that was stuck in the player. She laughed and nodded.

"Okay. I'll come over at half eight."

I tried not to watch her leave, but she simply consumed my attention. After finishing my coffee, I followed suit and rode around town for a while, blowing out the cobwebs and chasing the wind, hoping for some answers to hit me like an epiphany. Nothing came to me however, so I went home. Mom was out (which was unusual for her) and I ended up in my studio.

Before I knew what was happening, I was scrawling a frenzy onto the canvas.

*** *** ***

The next morning I opened my eyes to the intoxicating smell of a good strong coffee.

"Hi. Y'know, you sleep real deep," Malena said, looking puzzled as she studied me.

"How did you get in?" I asked, bolting upright and staring at the door I thought I'd locked.

"I knocked a few times and could see you through the window but I got worried when you didn't wake up. The door was open so I just let myself..."

"The door was open?" I interrupted, stumbling over to the window. Now that I thought about it I couldn't remember closing the drapes and had clearly been too engrossed in sketching to worry about security either. Sloppy, considering I had a crazy doppelganger after me...

Yes. She was coming for me. Her *esta* had been approved and she'd booked her flight for tonight while I slept. That meant I had today and tomorrow to prepare for her.

"Nikki? You okay? I'm sorry if I freaked y'all out by just coming on in but I panicked when I saw you and...you sleep REAL deep, y'know?" Malena repeated and I turned to stare at her.

"It's okay, I'm not freaked out by you. I...I have a sleep condition that means I sleep for exactly twelve hours every night and nothing can wake me. I just normally lock the door is all." I mumbled, trying to get my head around the ticking time bomb approaching. But because Malena still looked upset and was still holding out the take-out coffee cup to me, I forced a tight smile onto my face. "Bad dreams. When I'm having a nightmare it means I'm stuck in it and can't wake up, no matter how bad."

"Fuck. That must be awful. Do you get them a lot?"

I took the coffee from her and shut my eyes as I took a gulp of the now lukewarm fluid.

"Pretty much every night, but they've got a lot worse lately. Like Fred Krueger worse."

"Is there anything I can do to help?"

I shivered. It all felt very fucking real now — too real.

"You already do sweetie." I checked the clock on the wall although I knew it would be just a few minutes past seven forty-one, the same time I woke every single day. Ness would be here in forty-five minutes.

"Did you draw this?" Malena asked, standing in front of my newest piece and regarding it with the same puzzled expression she'd been wearing when I woke up. I stood next to her and exhaled deeply as I took it in, the dark lines of a large contorted self-portrait where one side appeared to be screaming in agony and the other in fury. It was a clever piece, but I detested every stroke of the charcoal.

"Yes, I did."

"It's dark."

"It's my nightmare."

She took my hand shyly and gave it a gentle squeeze, her eyes catching mine briefly then skittering away. I flushed with unexpected heat. What was it about this girl that affected me so much? Hoping I didn't have terrible morning breath, I pulled her round and cupped her cheeks in my palms, moving in for a kiss. Evidently not caring what my breath was like, she pressed her soft lips against mine, her body melting against mine, her tongue tangling with mine. Our pants were pulled open in a flurry as the kissing intensified and when I slid my fingers into her she groaned loudly as if it was some kind of elixir she'd been craving for a long time. My clit pulsed in time with hers as I thrust into her, and when she managed to twist her hand between my legs I gasped loudly, unable to stop my eyes rolling. She pushed me to the wall, biting and sucking at sensitive areas of my neck and with a few quick moves on her part, brought me to a loud climax. Hers followed not long after while I was still riding my wave and I watched her flushed face as she came round. We stared at each other as our ragged breathing steadied.

69

"I think I'm close to fallin' for you."

The whispered words sounded scared and she looked like she might burst into tears at any second.

"Ditto."

We fell into a hug, gripping and holding on as if our lives depended on it. Truth of the matter was...I actually felt like I was falling for her, and it did scare me. Lord only knew how she must have been feeling. Eventually we moved apart and did up our pants, almost embarrassed at our joint confession.

"So, I came over to ask if you'd come with me to see Pop. Y'know...obviously not see her, but..."

"Sure. I promised to take Ness to her rehearsal first though. Can I meet you at about ten and go then?" As I said this I watched closely for her reaction, expecting her to blow up or lose her shit again, but she just tucked some loose strands of hair behind her ear and nodded. We agreed on a neutral place to meet up, I thanked her for the coffee, and just like that she was gone. It was still only five to eight.

I went indoors and showered before Ness arrived and when I came back down, found mom scowling at me from the kitchen.

"You, young lady, have a lot to answer for."

"Huh? What'd I do now?"

"You know full and well what I mean. They..." she dropped her voice to a hushed whisper, "...they run a house of sin over there, and you've been getting involved with them!"

"Oh for Pete's sake mom, it's not what you think! I don't know what you've heard but it's wrong."

"We had a street meeting last night over at Phil's house and we think if we can get enough signatures on a petition, we can maybe force them out!"

"You...what? Who? What are you talking about?" I spluttered, feeling my stress levels elevate even further.

"About half the block turned up to discuss the extra-curricular activities of that house and we all made a unified decision that we weren't going to just sit back and let them corrupt our community with their sinful ways."

"What? Why would you do that? They just want to be left alone. Sheesh mom, this is the twenty-first century, not the middle ages! Did you know their daughter, Ness, is competing in ice dancing at a National level soon? She's just as normal as you and me."

I could tell mom didn't care if Ness was an International pop star with ten number one singles under her belt — she wasn't a God fearing child and that meant she would never be as normal as us (although I'd never been any kind of normal but I guess she was able to overlook it because I was under her careful watch.)

"Nikki, they are conducting themselves in a very loose manner and this is one community that is not just gonna sit back and let the darkness spread through like a disease. Something has to be done and WILL be done." She pursed her lips to mark the end of the discussion, just as there was a knock at the door. Jutting out my chin defiantly I said,

"That'll be Ness. I'm taking her to the rink and I will talk to you later — we are not done here." And with that I grabbed my keys and lids and stalked out, slamming the door behind me. I was ashamed of my own mother, enough so that I couldn't tell Ness what had just occurred. To give Ness her dues, she didn't question me on why I was so angry — she simply pulled the lid over her head and climbed quietly on the back of my bike while I revved far too much torque out of the engine. I wanted to gun it out of there, but Ness's arms around my waist were a calming influence and I pulled my shit together enough to not burn rubber.

"I'm sorry about that. It's my mom, she's trying to spearhead a campaign I don't agree with," I explained when we reached our destination and I was able to form words without spitting.

"And Nick's *esta* came through — she's gonna be flying out tonight, so my guess is that she'll be here tomorrow night."

"Oh, shit. I wasn't expecting it to happen this quick."

"Me neither." I scratched my head, feeling the heat moistening my hair even at this early hour. For some reason, I had the irrational thought that it was blood and not sweat and I found myself checking my fingertips but there was no sign of red. I exhaled slowly. "Look, please don't let this affect you. I don't want you losing focus on your skating because of me, okay? I feel like a grade A shit for even bringing it up now."

"Don't worry, I'll be fine. Skating's kinda like my way of getting shit outta my system so it might even help my performance," she reassured. "You coming in or shooting off?"

"I said I'd go with Malena to Poppy's grave but I'd like to come by after if that's okay?" She nodded and jogged towards the side entrance for the rink, giving a quick wave before disappearing inside.

*** *** ***

"Pop was always the one had it easy. I reckon part of that was cos she just didn't give a fuck about what anyone thought," Malena laughed quickly, then sobered up again almost instantly when it threatened to turn into a sob. "I always envied her. I kinda hated her because I wanted it to be that easy for me too, but I cared too much what people thought about me. I always wanted mom and dad's approval and goddammit I had to work so freakin' hard to get it. I guess all that hard work just made me uptight and resentful." She sniffed and looked at her hands twisting together in her lap. "You wanna hear something that's real fucked up? When I was about thirteen, I told Pop I liked girls, y'know, more'n I liked boys. A couple a years later, she came out and told mom and dad she thought she was gay. I was so angry with her for copying me, and for having the strength I didn't have to come out...so I just bottled it all up and pretended I was straight. I felt like she'd done it on purpose or something and I carried all this secret resentment around for years. Don't get me wrong, I loved Poppy more'n anything — aside from being my sister it was near on impossible not to, you know? But deep inside...I hated her."

"She was leading the life you wanted." I said quietly. She nodded.

"And when she died, I realised I didn't hate her at all...I hated myself for not being stronger, for not going out and getting what I wanted. And now she's gone..." Malena hesitated, looking guiltily at the ground in front of us as if Poppy might rise from the coffin below and claw her way up, "...now she's gone I feel like I've got my life back. I can be all the things I wanted to be. Why is that?"

I swallowed uncomfortably. Was this how Nick felt about me? Beneath the dark fury and bitter resentment was she just someone struggling with life because she got dealt a different hand? If she managed to kill me would she feel free and be able to live the life she'd always craved?

"I don't know. Do you think you coulda come to this point if she hadn't died though? I mean, couldn't you both have lived the lives you both wanted without hating each other?"

"I would never have explored my sexuality. It was bad enough for mom and dad that one daughter was gay — I'd never have broken them by admitting I was too so I just kinda settled, looked for guys who were timid and quiet and didn't want much from me. As for Pop, well she never hated on me at all. She was always happy, woulda done anything for me, you know? She was the perfect sister." She looked me in the eye. "It's shitty, right? I feel like all the hatred and resentment dissolved when she died and I was left with sadness and pain...but I was also reborn and I felt free."

We stayed at Poppy's graveside for another hour, occasionally talking but mostly thinking, deep in thought. I felt more confused than ever, but now at least I had a clearer understanding of Nick and her motivation for getting rid of me. I just didn't know if I'd be able to do anything to persuade her not to.

I managed to catch a couple of hours of Ness skating, but it was enough to soothe the jagged lines around my soul. She was dancing to three songs for the scout, feeling the difference in tempos would be able to highlight as many of her abilities and skills as possible. The first was an old Tina Arena tune, *'Chains'* where the song built up from a gentle ballad to a passionate plea. The powerful words brought me out in goosebumps and I felt extra chilled to the bone as I listened to them. The second song was an old Aretha Franklin one, *'Think'* and it raised the tempo up as Ness swooped and dove around the ice. The final song was a beautiful classic — *'Time To Say Goodbye'*. Something about her song choices bothered me deeply, but I knew she hadn't based them on my situation so it must've just been a coincidence.

Whatever I thought about her reasoning for choosing them, they were excellent choices and I couldn't envisage the scout not being completely entranced by how she dominated the ice. Ness had a way of owning your attention before you noticed it had been stolen.

Before we went home she let me buy her dinner at an excellent seafood restaurant I knew and I told her about my conversation with Malena. She agreed how similar the situations seemed.

We rode home, both of us remarkably relaxed considering what lay ahead of us the next day, and when I found Malena was waiting for me at my door, a shy smile on her face, I couldn't help but feel a surge of contentment.

I didn't want the day to end, but I knew it had to. One thing was for sure — no matter what happened tomorrow, today had been pretty perfect.

What should you do on your potentially final day alive?

I spent the morning (and some of the afternoon) making love with Malena and for lunch we ordered a pizza that was big enough to feed a family of ten. She left at three, giving me plenty of time to freshen up and get down to the rink for five. Because Wednesdays were quite quiet anyway, and the scout was a pretty big deal to happen here in Saloam Springs, they'd closed up for the evening to give Ness total freedom and concentration. I mean let's face it, if she got into Nationals, this place would make the headlines so it was worth losing a few bucks tonight.

I walked in through the private side entrance feeling incredibly nervous. Amanda and Kev were here already, standing at the edge of the ice and chatting to a lady who could only be the revered scout while Ness glided around the ice, doing a few little jumps and spins to warm up. I nodded to Amanda — she smiled warmly and waved back. No hard feelings there then.

As I took a seat in the stands, I wondered where Nick was. Her flight would be ready to land soon and then...it was showtime for us. I was no closer to working out a plan to pacify her — I HAD debated offering her the small fortune I had put away, but could tell that wouldn't be enough for her. She wanted all or nothing and this world wasn't big enough for the two of us.

After what seemed like an agonisingly long wait, Amanda and Kev came to sit with me. The scout, a lady in her early forties, went to find her own viewing spot. I could barely breathe! Ness got into position on the ice and everything went quiet...

"This is so surreal. I still can't believe...did she say what I thought she said or did I imagine it?"

"Depends. If you thought she said it was one of the most superb performances she'd ever come to watch on a non-International level then no, you heard right," I said, smiling proudly. Ness and I were sitting on a makeshift picnic blanket on the ice and eating a large bag of potato chips and various bars of candy. The janitor had left Ness in charge of locking up after we left, letting us celebrate in a nice quiet fashion on our own.

"I know it might sound weird but I didn't actually believe I had a chance. I'm going through to National level Nikki! OH MY GOD!" Ness threw herself back onto the ice and screamed her elation, the noise echoing round the empty rink. I laughed and chucked a square of chocolate at her mouth but hit her ear instead. She laughed back and fished it out of her hair, throwing it back. She was glowing — she was sublime.

"I'm think I'm in love with Malena but I think I'm falling for you too," I blurted, unable to stop myself. Ness looked up at me, still smiling.

"No, you're not."

"What do you mean?"

"I mean no, you're not falling in love with me. You're just confused is all."

"Yes, I am."

"How many friends do you have, Nikki?"

"What? What's that got to do with it?"

"Because you don't really have any, do you? As far as I can tell, you just have lots of girlfriends but no actual friends that you don't sleep with. You and I, we connect very easily, right? I think maybe you're just mistaking our *friend* connection for a romantic one because you've never had it before," Ness explained patiently. I stared at her, dumb for a minute as I took it in and chewed it over. "C'mon Nikki, even if I was gay, we'd never make it as a couple, and you know that, deep in your heart. But as friends...we can go a long way."

She was right. I knew she was right. And she knew I knew she was right because she laughed again. "I can't believe you're a friend virgin!"

I laughed at the absurdity and truth of her comment.

"You're like my first! Does that mean you're gonna break my heart?"

"I'll try not to. Usually the job of a friend is to help mend them with ice cream and hugs after a horrible break-up though."

My heart warmed — I had a new girlfriend and a best friend all in the space of a day. Even as I was starting to glow myself, I suddenly noticed the time — it was two minutes to my pass-out time.

"Shit! Oh...shit, I've only got two minutes!" I said, jumping awkwardly to my feet. "Is there anywhere I can crash until the morning?"

"We could go to the viewing box? Follow me, I'll bring blankets after I've shown you where it is!" Ness said running carefully across the ice. She took me to a box that had a large floor to ceiling window, offering a perfect view of the entire rink.

"Wow!"

"I'll stay here with you if you want? Make sure you're okay? The doors are all locked downstairs."

"Are you sure she wouldn't be able to get in?"

I didn't hear her reply as I fell to the floor.

CHAPTER TWELVE

My memories of being young are few and far between. In fact, I have very few memories at all. My mind is like a sieve that sometimes holds on to a thought or an image or a dream and I try to make it into sense. That's been the way of my life for as long as I am able to recall. These jumbled pieces of glass that thrown together might make a beautiful coloured window, seem in my mind, a puzzle where I cannot quite move the pieces to the correct place. And if I could, I would have the window in a church where worshippers would fall to their knees and weep at the beauty.

After I had spoken to Mr Chan, I phoned the Norwegian stunner who lived below me. I am going to be honest now before it is too late. That Freya *is* a stunner, she *is* gorgeous. She brought some kind of life into my dead heart before Helena returned and I cannot forget that. There are things I cannot remember and there are things I wish I could forget.

Life is a fine line between dreams and memories, wishes and hopes. Step the wrong way and you could be knee-deep in a love that doesn't belong to your heart. I am treading my way through the treacle footsteps that hinder me, all the while my heart is raging forward. Therein lies my problem. If my heart didn't rage, then neither would I. I am held — torn, suspended — with my love for Helena and the dream of someone else who might tear me away from this life.

A hand slaps me.

The harsh pain brings me back to life. I swallow, as my eyes look around, gaining their knowledge from the familiarity of surroundings.

"WHO THE FUCK AM I?" I scream.

I begin to cry because a broken heart will show itself first from the eyes and you have to look closer to see the signs of heartache. Only one broken heart can recognise another. Pain reaches out to make a sibling of its ache, searching for some comfort.

Every sorrow seeks a mirror.

"Sh," she says, her soft fingers stroking my hair, bringing me close. I shut my eyes, scared to see what torture love would lay before me.

"I could love you," I whisper, my heart beating like a tattered old drum.

"You *do* love me," she whispered back, her cool voice laying ice over the fears that were taking root in my mind. "And that's the reason you will leave me."

My big, fat gob shut itself as I took in the words she said.

"Oh," she sighed. "You have to leave me."

"What?"

"You have to leave me."

Freya took my face in her hands, her eyes wide with tears and I found I could see my soul as I looked into her.

Every mirror seeks a sorrow.

Pain makes sorrow the happiest emotion. Each tug of my heart, that had seemed so hard, so sure of its meaning, falls away into nothing. There are no happy pulls.

I shake my head, knowing somewhere below I am capable of happiness if I am allowed. All the while Freya is holding me in her arms, whispering words to me in a language that I don't understand but that somehow soothes me nevertheless. How can I be soothed by someone who is not Helena?

I pant into her, holding her close, floundering in the tumult of emotions that truth brings to me. There is a saying that the truth hurts but I don't agree. It's the lies that have disguised the truth that cause the problems.

I have been an expert at hiding my truths, at turning my emotions into angers that seemed more agreeable. Anger is easier to deal with than love. Every emotion is easier to deal with than love. It is the only thing that terrifies, from teenage to old age. Because no-one wants to be wrong. No-one wants to feel a fool. Who is this unworthy sloth that I have given my heart to? Why did I not see this?

I watch the dagger edge closer and closer to me, to stab the desire from my stupid heart that never learns.

Freya still holds me tight, demanding that my eyes meet hers and, as hard as I try, I have to meet them eventually.

Love will always out.

And when I see her eyes, those pools of bright blue, I forget the horrors of my heart. I forget that love can also take horrors and throw them aside. I begin to swim in her and my shattered mind finds a piece of happiness it can hold on to.

Freya, I think, not sure where a thought can lead me.

Nicki, I remember, teeth clenched in hate.

Helena, my jaw slackens in misery.

There is so much to see and feel and I cannot be sure where I am supposed to look and see. All my life, I have been wrapped inside a box, too scared to peek out, terrified Nikki would bat me down.

No wonder an emotion is the scariest thing in my world, when my world only consists of emotions that don't belong to me. Finding myself in an ocean of thoughts is almost impossible.

I grit my teeth.

I hold Freya to me. I take in the rhythmic beat of her heart and let it reassure me. She has never once swayed. Her love has been steadfast.

I feel myself sink, knowing Freya is right when she said I would leave her.

True loves never end up together. Like Heathcliff and Cathy, we shall be separated by the vain love of others.

My fingers itch to feel Helena. But when my hand stretches out all I can feel is the soft, coolness of Freya. Her skin is like poetry to my reading fingers.

I pull myself away, running to my bathroom where I can splash water to my face, hoping I will be brought back to myself because I don't feel like I am someone I know anymore.

My face touches the porcelain and I breathe in the cold water splashes my hands are fanning to my face. I raise my head and look in the mirror at my reflection. My blue eyes meet my blue eyes. A wave of recognition flows down my body like the tide rushing in. A wave washes over me as I stare harder.

And then I see it, my face shaking as the image alters the tiniest bit and I realise I am not looking at myself, I'm looking at Nikki. I am looking in my mirror and seeing Nikki look back. Her mouth opens as my scream begins.

We are the same.

*** *** ***

I take a broken heart with me wherever I go. It's been like that for as long as I am allowed to remember.

"I have Nikki address," Mr Chan had told me and the wheels of motion began to roll, like a train I was driving at full speed with no place to go but the end of a track that took me over the mountain's edge. I knew now where she lived and I had the money in my bank from the portrait of the dwarf. I had paid Mr Chan his fee without grumbling too much to his surprise and my own, and then I had phoned Ethel because I wanted more money. I didn't know how long I'd need to be away and I didn't want to rush things. Anticipation for me would be terror for Nikki.

Getting to her wasn't as easy as I had hoped. I'd tried to buy a flight but the paperwork flummoxed me because I wasn't as smart as Nikki. I had never been able to afford expensive holidays to exotic locations, so I didn't know the correct protocol. It was sheer chance I even had a passport.

With every second that passed, I felt my hatred grow for Nikki, my happiness thief.

I went to see Freya the night before I flew away. She had answered her door with such a sad look on her face and I felt my heart, already broken, shatter into a million pieces. I cannot abide a woman with tears in her eyes because it steals all the walls I have erected to protect myself. I held her in my arms for a long time, neither of us daring to speak, enjoying the moment we knew would be our last.

"When do you leave?" she asked finally.

"First thing in the morning," I told her.

"Will you come back?" she asked, struggling to hold the break that was trying to come through in her voice.

"I don't think so," I told her. "I don't know how this ends but it probably won't end well for me."

"Then stay this night with me," she demanded, holding me tighter in her arms as if she thought I might try to escape.

"I'll fall asleep," I told her. "But I'll stay. Hold me while I sleep."

"Jeg vil aldri gi slipp pa hjertet ditt."

I'd no idea what she meant as I drifted off but I hoped she would hold on to my heart.

*** *** ***

I was on a tight schedule and had no time to waste in the morning but I took a moment to kiss Freya goodbye. She had given my heart happiness when it was drowning in a sea of heartbreak. She had cooled the fires that Helena had set alight in me, the passion that almost consumed me, almost burned me out.

To free Freya and save her, I'd have to leave her, set her off to find love away from me.

"You go to your friend, Mavis Street," I told her, while my taxi waited, my hands on her face. "You tell her I've had to leave and that you need a friend. She loves you. She'll look after you in a way I'd never be able to."

She nodded, tears making pathways on her face, glistening in the strain of sunlight.

"I love you," I told her. "I love you!" I said again, through gritted teeth. "It's taken a lifetime to show me this. It's too late for me but it's not too late for you. Don't be dragged down like I was. Find a love, be happy. Live in happiness."

She kissed me.

And that was all we could do for each other now because the kiss between us had always been everything and always would be. A kiss is for life. The music from Freya's lips fed through me, into my ears, my heart, and made me dance to her tune.

Too late, too late, I was always too late.

I wasn't going to be late anymore. For Nikki, I was going to be right on time to end her. But I was saving Freya and that made it worthwhile. To make the right choice at the end seemed worthwhile. Something surely had to be.

I was saving Freya from the torture that the love for Helena held around me, I was shackled with the chains around my ankles dancing to the tune Helena wanted. I had been held in these chains for years, it was all slowly making sense the closer I came to meeting Nikki.

It was like I had been laid a trail of gingerbread crumbs and the more I ate them through life, the closer I got to my destiny.

Our destiny, I reminded myself.

Nikki might be laying out the crumbs but I was gobbling them up as if I was starving. I was the pecking hen grubbing for the shit she'd throw me. I was and always had been desperate for her crumbs.

No more! I'd had enough of her rubbish. I fell asleep between my perfectly organised flights, the ones it had given me a headache to arrange, agonising over the details, time differences, sleep patterns. But I kept going because I would no longer let that bitch beat me.

Freya, Freya, Helena, Helena. Two of everything.

The women I loved, spinning around my head as I boarded my plane. The slut had been at it again while I was making my way over. She wouldn't know the difference between love and lust if they slapped her in the face. The only things she liked slapped in her face were another's thighs. She revolted me.

I never touched a woman unless I thought it could lead to love. If it didn't lead to love, it was just lust and I am not an animal, I can wait, I can control myself. I *will* wait. I waited ten years for Helena, only to realise in the moment of our love, that she would never be what I had yearned for. That was the most heartbreaking part of it all. Not her betrayal or her inability to trust in me years ago, or her marrying a man. It was the knowing I was wrong, that I had given my heart to the wrong lover. Who wants to hear that they have been deceived by the very organ they hold most dear?

It's like looking into the mirror and seeing a reflection that could kill you. A face that is yours but not yours. A heart that beats inside a rib cage that feels like it's your own but is someone else's love. A spiteful love that wants you to suffer burning inside, a mirror image that wants to torture and torment, taking any form of happiness away from that heart that could have been theirs.

I've looked into a mirror and seen a world change before my eyes. I've seen love change to misery, and misery change to love. I've felt hands hold me down to heartache and weights pull me under trying to drown me in feelings that weren't meant for me. I have looked at love with happiness and sadness, with longing and hatred. I have looked behind love and in front of it and I'm still no closer to understanding the mystery that makes it twist around me, knowing I want it out of me. I want rid of this, this atrocity that strikes me when I am weak, that gives me strength when I think I have none and then winds me once more, a laughter echoing far away.

Love, love, I wanted you so much. I ached for you. I longed to feel you in my toes and on the hairs that stood on my arms in the cold. I was desperate with my heartbeat, hoping love would hear me. I heard every sad song and knew it had been written for me.

"Love! Love! Find me!" I screamed in so many nightmares that, when I opened my eyes, were there in that day. Sunlight never hid my fears.

I held what I thought was love close to me for so many years that now it felt like some titanic joke the universe had played on me. I hadn't held love — I had held fear.

There was only one of us that had love and that was Nikki. She had taken the love meant for us both and claimed it all for herself, unable to share, unable to give me a tiny shred of happiness. I was coming for her and, as I thought this, I felt the tears fall down my face.

I was hurting. It hurt too much but I wouldn't stop. I wasn't going to end until one of us had ended.

I fell asleep in a hotel room. I woke up and it made me smile that Nikki was terrified because she knew I was here.

Destiny had brought me to her. There were songs that had been written about us that if you listened you'd hear, they take your heart and toss it in the air before kicking it away.

But I had things to do today and feeling sorry for myself was not one of them. I had limited time, as both Nikki and I were well aware of, and I quickly pulled on my jeans, boots and jumper. I brushed my teeth, splashed some water on my face, running my wet hands through my hair. I didn't want to look in the mirror, too scared by what horror might greet me, and I didn't mean the state of my reflection.

I meant eyes that would lock with mine, taking all I had. I used to feel that looking at Helena drained me because the emotions I felt from her tired me out, over-powered me but it was just another lie, told to keep me in my chains. Only one of us could be happy, I saw that.

I lit a cigarette as soon as I left the hotel, walking fast and smoking, enjoying the slight dizziness the nicotine brought. When I finished smoking, I hailed a taxi and gave the driver the address Mr Chan had provided me with.

I stared out the window, my heart calm now that the final minutes were ticking down. I didn't see the houses and cars and people that we passed. It was a blur, my eyes looking somewhere else in time.

The taxi stopped, I looked at the meter and paid, adding a tip because I had heard Americans expected it and I didn't want him to think the Scottish were mean, even though I wouldn't normally tip someone just for doing their job.

I was stood in a quiet street, houses facing houses, lawns and well-watered trees littering the avenue. The sun was high in the sky and I took my jumper off, tying it around my waist. Now that I was here, I didn't quite know what I was going to do, so I lit another cigarette.

As I blew out my first inhale, slipping my Zippo lighter back into my jean's pocket, I saw a woman leaving and locking a side door on the smaller building attached to the house I was standing in front of. Of course, Nikki had her own private studio. Nikki had fucking everything.

As I lifted my cigarette to bring it to my lips, the woman turned down the path, walking towards me, my cigarette frozen in mid-air.

"Helena?" I squeaked. "What are you doing here?"

"Nikki?" the woman said, a confused look on her face.

She looked so much like my Helena! She continued to scrutinise me as I realised what she had said. She had called me Nikki and I realised then that I must, to an outsider, look like a version of Nikki. A skinny, bedraggled scruffy version but eyes that reflected in a mirror.

"You're not Nikki," she half laughed, in the American twang I was still getting used to. "You look so like her but the accent is wrong. I'm Malena," she added, almost as an after-thought.

"Hello, Malena. I'm a friend of Nikki's from the UK. Is she in?" I asked, finally remembering the cigarette burning my fingers.

Burning, burning, someone was going to burn. But no, not her.

She looked me up and down suspiciously.

"We blog together about our paintings," I told her, suddenly vocal. "She's better off than I am," I laughed. "But she invited me over, said we would paint together, a fusing of styles she called it." The lies and smiles fell together easily.

I looked at Malena closer as I spoke. Her eyes, her face, they...they were so like Helena it disarmed me. Ten minutes ago, I would've stabbed anyone who stood between me and Nikki, but no, I couldn't hurt Malena.

Malena, Helena. It was all too close to home.

I must have convinced her because all at once she smiled a warm, Helena-style smile and I thought my heart would break once more, when I had thought there was nothing left to break. Beautiful women have always been my enemy.

"She's gone to the rink with Ness, I actually thought she'd be back by now," she said, as if I knew who Ness was.

"Oh, damn," I said, slapping my forehead. "I still can't get used to this time difference. Where's the ice rink? I'd love to surprise her. Can you tell me where it is? Oh, she will love this!" I exclaimed, my sheer excitement, winning her over.

"Here," she said, taking her phone from her pocket to show me where to go.

"Thank you! And could you get me an Uber, my phone doesn't work here," I smiled, wanting to touch her and not knowing if that touch was to caress or kill.

"Of course!" she grinned. "You've come so far, judging by your accent. I'll do anything for a friend of Nikki."

She ordered me an Uber and we haggled over payment, as I left throwing a ten dollar bill at her. God, you wouldn't get this aggro in Glasgow.

As I sat silent in the back of yet another cab, I wondered why Nikki would pick a woman to fall in love with who was the replica of the girl I had fallen in love with as a teenager. What had attracted her to a woman who looked *exactly* like the girl I'd been obsessed with for years? Was she seeing something in my love that she wanted for herself? That would be typical of her, hating me, getting one over on me, wanting what I had. By choosing Malena, she had saved her life. I'd never hurt someone who looked like Helena, even though I knew her love was no longer right for me. Memories are powerful things that can conjure up an image of a lost love at the drop of an eyelid.

In that second my hands could have been around Malena's neck as quickly as it was Helena's and then I would have been horrified.

Who was who?

Who is who and who am I?

I had no time to wonder as my taxi dropped me off at the ice rink where Nikki was with some girl called Ness. Did she love her? I felt my anger begin to rise. Did she love her like I had loved Helena for all those years, hopelessly waiting for a woman who would never love me the way I wanted to be loved, because all my love had been stolen before I could have it by a jealous slag?

Nikki didn't know what it felt like to lose the one you loved. Oh sure, she'd slept with her fair share of women, I think one had even died, but she'd never had her heart twisted and tortured under a turning heel that squashed it down. She didn't know the utter desolation of a lonely life, where love passed you by and all you had to hold on to were memories and dreams that would never come true.

That was it.

Nikki had never known how I felt but it was too late for retrospective pity, as I searched for a way in to the locked ice rink. I wandered the boundary seeing a light on and I knew, *I just knew*, that Nikki was in there, trying to hide. The doors were locked but, growing up in Glasgow had taught me a thing or two, and I soon found a way in. I listened for any tiny sound as I made my way to the centre, where the rink was, and I crept around until I saw them, wrapped around each other. Two bodies, with smiles on their faces, their arms and legs tight together.

I stood for a moment, finally seeing Nikki in front of me. I looked at her thin legs, so fragile, her skinny arms grabbing the girl I assumed was Ness, trying to hold her body over her, never knowing what horrors might come in her sleep.

A horror like me.

A tear slipped down my cheek. I loved Nikki and she would never know this. I'd never tell her that when my heart beat I felt hers too, that when she cried, I felt a tear behind my eye. She would have hated my love. She did everything to take love away from me.

She took it all away.

I looked at her, eyes closed, and I closed mine. I let the darkness join us, I heard my heart beat with hers and I heard an echo of her fears. "Don't hurt her," she said.

I grabbed the girl that lay on top of Nikki by her hair and I dragged her, as she woke up, arms flailing. I kicked her, again and again.

"Stop screaming!" I told her. "She can't hear you."

"Don't hurt her," whispered in my mind. I gritted my teeth, tightening the grip of my fist on her hair as I continued dragging her on to the ice, trying my best not to slide.

"Shut up screaming, you little bitch!" I shouted as I felt her nails dig in to my calves. She was strong for a wee, skinny lassie. I brought my foot down on her knee, hearing a crack as she screamed in pain.

I looked at her and felt nothing. I began to punch her in the face, over and over, again and again, my fist declaring its pain as I slipped in the blood from her nose and mouth with every blow.

When I felt my finger break, I stopped and I looked at the inert face of the young girl I had pummelled. I left her unconscious and returned to Nikki's side.

It's not the first time I have been filled with sadness but I knew Nikki wouldn't understand that. She hated me and I'd make her hate me more. I'd had enough of living a half-life.

This was it. This was my chance to kill Nikki. No more jealousy, no more stealing my happiness, no more of her in my head. I lifted an ice skate and lowered it until the blade touched her neck, kneeling beside her sleeping body. I saw her quiet, smiling face, so peaceful in a sleep that couldn't hurt her and I pressed the blade against her throat until I could see a red line begin.

I thought of all the love I'd had in my life, I saw the first moment Helena smiled at me and my breath froze in my throat. I felt Nikki loving someone else whose name I'd never know. I tried to press the blade and I was filled with the touches Helena's soft fingers had made on me that melted my cruel heart.

Who was it that had the cruel heart? My heart was never cruel and Nikki...Nikki...I glared at her and tried to hate her but I couldn't press the blade on her throat any harder. I felt the familiar choke in my throat, as the years of unhappiness weighed me down, filling me with regrets. My eyes were blinded by tears as I stared at Nikki, removing the blade from her neck.

I ran a finger across the red line I'd left on her skin, her pretty face oblivious in our deep sleep.

I love her.

I leant over and put my lips on hers, so soft that only a wind would know that we had touched. I got up quickly picking up the ice skate and I returned to the body that could have been me unconscious.

I had no trouble pressing my blade to the girl's throat and I watched, in sheer fascination as the blood spread quickly from her throat across the ice, her scared eyes wide as she realised too late that she was dying.

Whoever she was. She wasn't me. She wasn't Nikki. I couldn't kill Nikki: it'd be like killing myself.

The red blood spread on the white ice, it was beautiful and I admired the luxury of colour. I took my hand and I made a message, red against white that only Nikki would understand. Then I ran to my hotel room and I waited for my sleep. I waited for Nikki to wake up.

I might not be able to kill her but I could kill her heart.

CHAPTER THIRTEEN

In the movies blood is always a vibrant bright red, which any idiot knows is completely inaccurate. If you cut your finger the blood starts out that way for sure, but after about twenty minutes to an hour it dries and goes a deep crimson or even a nasty brown. It's something that niggles me a lot when I'm watching slasher films — the blood stays bright red for hours and hours, sometimes even days.

Ness's blood, however, had stayed that way, frozen in a fantastic display of red swirls on white ice. I was transfixed by the macabre beauty below and too numb to answer any questions poised by whoever was stood behind me. The cops had just arrived and I knew they weren't holding me as a suspect. Obviously when I wouldn't wake, and with a slither of red juice escaping my own neck, they initially assumed they were dealing with two bodies.

Ness. Her life had just started to blossom with opportunity and my bastard twin had simply erased her out of, what, spite? Because she could? Because she fucking wanted to? Was I doomed to see every woman I loved die in such horrific ways? She didn't know the meaning of losing a love! Oh, she proclaimed to have a love for Helena that surpassed the boundaries of any heart, but she'd never known how it felt to really lose her. Not in the same way I knew about loss...

Time was short. I had to get out of here as quickly as possible. I gave a brief statement to the cops, saying I had no idea who had attacked us. They were familiar with my condition so I was cleared almost immediately. The good thing about having such a rare disorder in a small town was how quickly news spread within the medical community. Occasionally I'd been caught short and woken up in hospital to be monitored, so all the EMTs around here knew of me. They verified my condition to the cops and I was allowed to go home alone after insisting I could ride my bike.

I was focused. I was a goddamn arrow of such intensity I was burning a trail of bitter black ash in my wake. My hatred for *her* was like an icy furnace, the flames lapping away at my insides and consuming everything within their path. She'd wanted to kill my heart and she'd succeeded — now residing in its place was a screaming darkness. What did she expect me to do? Go after her? The little book of matches she'd left in my pocket were a bold message telling me where she was — like a dare for me to face her as she'd faced me. Well, I had a much better plan, one she was not going to like in the slightest, but I had to move fast.

The street was teeming with cop cars and if I wasn't mistaken, a news van had already arrived on the scene. I wanted in and out in no longer than five minutes. I would not, could not speak to anyone. I ran into the house, ignoring mom's cries, found my passport and cash, then I was out the door and on my bike, trying to pretend the screams of pain and anguish coming from Amanda's house were all in my imagination.

I rode like the devil was chasing me out of hell to find the Motel she'd holed up in, skidding into the parking lot and losing a good portion of rubber from the wheels as I did so. I ran into the reception and asked the idiot behind the counter which room Nick was in. At first he resisted giving me any information until I hinted she'd just checked in yesterday, was about to kill herself and I needed to stop her. That was enough of a jolt up his ass, he gave me a spare key and went back to watching the show on the box that I'd interrupted, leaving me to face my doppelganger alone.

I stood over her, curious. She looked surprisingly peaceful but the hatred that I felt for her only intensified at this. She didn't deserve to be at peace, ever. I wanted to kill her, to rip her apart piece by hateful piece until I'd exposed her dark heart, then I would squeeze it until it popped between my fingers.

I sat on her chest, my hands tightening around her throat. Her body squirmed slightly beneath me as I denied her the air she needed. Oh, the temptation to finish her off right now was strong and nearly overwhelming, but I forced myself to relinquish my hold on her life. Breathing heavily as I regained my control, I lowered my face down until we were mere inches away — I could smell her sour darkness emanating from every rank pore.

Enough. I jumped to my feet and turned the room upside down until I found what I was looking for — some ID with her home address on, her phone and a set of keys. The thumbprint security was easy to bypass with her right next to me and I set about changing the security so I'd be able to access it without her — I was going to need her keys when I got to the UK and I didn't want her able to warn anyone I was coming. The phone might come in handy at some point.

Tulsa International airport was about a hundred and twenty kilometres away and I got there in just over thirty-five minutes. There was no fear in me as I'd pushed my bike to extreme limits of speed, feeling almost guided by unseen forces. I left my trusty machine outside the main entrance of the airport, keys in the ignition and still purring, and ran to the ticket desk. As if fate were on my side, there was a flight to Glasgow leaving in ninety minutes and I managed to book a seat, arrange a special wheelchair for me to exit the plane, race to the gate and give over my ticket with just seconds to spare. It was six pm when I left American soil for the last time. Hopefully I wouldn't need to be wheeled off the flight, but I wasn't sure about the different time zones.

My mind was black; blank. When it came time for my eyes to close, I explained my condition thoroughly to the hostess, making sure they understood not to panic and that I'd wake up (hopefully) just before we landed. But just in case, I was going to sleep in the wheelchair so they could remove me from the plane and not cause any hold ups for them.

I was utterly numb. Why had she done this to me? I just wanted everything to end and the only way to do that was to destroy her — perhaps in destroying each other something would just snap and one (or neither) of us would emerge victorious.

I woke as the plane was descending, much to the pleasure of the cabin crew. With no luggage to collect, I sailed through passport control and went straight to the taxi rank. It was going to be expensive getting to her place, but this was a one way trip and I had the funds at my disposal. I ignored the efforts of the driver to make polite chit chat but gave him a large tip when we arrived at the building she called home. I strode inside with her keys, never losing my focus for a second. There wasn't much to search — her flat was derelict and barren and I found what I was looking for within minutes.

Helena's address and phone number, stuck on the fridge door. It was almost too easy.

I needed to plug her phone in and let it charge briefly before I could send a text, begging Helena to come and see me before nightfall. If she said no, I'd just have to go to her, but things would work better if she came here.

"Nick, where have you been? I'll try to get out but I can't promise. Wait for me, I'll get to you when I can."

I read the message, sneering as I imagined how her face was going to look when she found us, Helena and I, tomorrow. She would be forced to make a decision and it would be the end either way. A certain amount of calm was beginning to settle over me at the thought and I moved around the cramped rooms as I waited for Helena to arrive.

She took her time and I actually started to worry she'd chickened out until I heard a confident knock on the door, which I'd left slightly ajar. Sure enough, when I didn't answer, the door swung slowly open and in stepped a girl. She was attractive — that much I could evaluate before the small baseball bat I was using as a club made contact with the side of her head. She crumpled easily and I dragged her in before realising she wasn't Helena. The long white hair gave her a Nordic appearance, but I was expecting company so I pulled her into the bedroom and checked her pulse. It was faint, but steady which gave me a good indication how hard to hit Helena when she arrived.

It was less than an hour before I was due to sleep when she finally walked in, calling out to Nick.

I hit her full in the face with my makeshift club and she stumbled back against the wall with the force of it. That was when I saw her swollen belly and something inside me hesitated. She really was pregnant!

What was I about to do?

For a split second, I reached out to help her, to see if she was all right and get medical aid for her...but then I remembered the red scene that had greeted my eyes not so long ago. I didn't know this woman, all I knew was that she was Nick's heart and soul and she had to be destroyed.

In silence, I swung at the lifeless form at my feet until I was certain there was no life left in it. Tears streamed down my face, but they too were silent. In contrast to the beauty of Ness's death, this was ugly, brutal.

I went back to the bedroom and stripped the blonde of her clothes, levering her up under the bedsheets. Then I stripped myself and lay next to her, somehow knowing this would be the cherry on the cake for my twin.

As my eyes closed, for perhaps the final time, I whispered one word.

"Nicola."

CHAPTER FOURTEEN

I woke up with my finger aching, unsure of where I was, what day it was, what life I was living. Then I felt the anguished beat of my heart, pumping the blood around that kept me alive, and with every throb, a memory became clearer.

I had killed an innocent girl. I hung my head in shame, the horror of what I had done filling me with regret. I couldn't kill Nikki but I should have let the girl Ness alone. My pain should not be Nikki's pain.

I got out of bed, feeling the unfamiliar heat of the sun warm through the closed curtains and I opened them to the dawn of a new day, a new day for me. Immediately I looked for my phone, knowing I had left it beside my bed as I always did and a panic set in as I saw it wasn't there. I got on my hands and knees to check under the bed, behind the bedside cabinet. Nothing. Nada.

I stripped the bed, telling myself it would be there, under a pillow or tangled down the covers. It had to be! It had to be somewhere. Unless…

I felt a weight on my chest and I lost my breath. I'd had a nightmare that Nikki had come into my room, filled with hate and rage, and she'd sat on me, debating my life and had come close to ending it, as I had with hers.

I stood up. I looked around the room, all my senses aware and I twitched my nose. She *had* been here! I could smell her! That had been no nightmare. That bitch *had* sat on me and made me squirm in a sleep I had no control over. I began to check all my belongings, knowing she would've stolen something. She knew then what I had done to Ness, she had found my message but she should have also seen that I spared her first. I could have killed her but I didn't. I had opened my eyes and let love find me because only love would save us.

I felt Nikki's pain in my bruised chest. I sat on the edge of my bed and I let myself be overtaken by all the emotions that I could no longer control. I felt the shame for what I had done to that wee lassie, Ness. She hadn't deserved that and I'd have the guilt eating away at me every day. There was never any thought for getting caught. I either did or I didn't and if the police in the USA had found their way to me, I'd have smiled and asked them to test my blood against Nikki's. I had no motive to kill a stranger but Nikki? She was sleeping with Malena and stringing along Ness. I knew who had more motive for that crime.

I smiled. She thought she was so clever. Her little tantrum in my room to let me know I'd gotten to her. I found myself laughing, until tears ran down my face and the tears became a river of sadness that I didn't know how to end. Tears and sadness are just the endless rivers that seem to run through me.

After a bit, I wiped the snot from my nose, throwing water on my face whilst careful to avoid the reflection in the mirror lest I see an image I didn't want to see. In my eyes is where fear begins. I don't want to be scared to live anymore.

I watched the sunset and I let my eyes close, knowing that when I opened them again everything would have changed and I'd be running for flights.

*** *** ***

I woke up in the arrivals lounge of Glasgow Airport and I relaxed, feeling the joy of being on Scottish home turf once more. Sometimes there is nothing that can made a heart jump with joy but knowing your feet are on the ground where you are safe.

I got my case and found a taxi to take me home. I knew Nikki had taken not only my phone but my keys. Freya had a spare set. I felt a bit giddy at the thought of seeing Freya again. I had not expected to return but then, I don't know what I had expected.

I thought of Freya. I imagined her delight when she opened the door to my knock, her white skin stretching into a smile that illuminated her beautiful face, curtained by her sweeping white hair. I wanted to kiss her. I wanted to take the soft skin of her face in my hands and bring her face close to mine. So close I'd never have to let her go.

But I *had* let her go. I had walked away to save her from the broken heart that loving me would no doubt entail. Wasn't that the best thing I could do for her? To know my love was wrong because love isn't always right. Love can be the worst thing in the world when two hearts don't collide.

And yet, and yet… my sorry heart could not stop from imagining a welcome Freya might give me. For her to hold me in her arms might be the acceptance I needed to move on from the hatred that Nikki planted in my heart. Only love can win in a heart frozen with hatred.

As I slipped back into the seat of my taxi, I closed my eyes, knowing this time I could control what I saw. And what I saw was Freya, her white-blonde pigtail centred down her back, waiting for my arms to encompass and hold her tight. I could almost feel the softness of her small breasts pushing into me, a pressure I found myself longing for.

I heard a whisper. A whisper of a life I could have had, a shadow of a dream that might still be possible. An echo of a heartbeat that sounded like a love story.

There's a way forward for me: a chance to be the person I want to be but… there's a chance I might end up as Nikki. I clenched my fists against that thought, knowing I was purer, I was worth living for, I was better than her.

I *have* to be.

And yet, and yet… I am no more nor no less her than I am myself.

I don't have time for this. I don't have time. I wait for my time.

*** *** ***

It's my day. It's my time to see where home will lead me. In my silly regime, I've had to sleep elsewhere before I have the guts to head home and see Freya because I don't want to see her and then fall away into an uncontrollable sleep.

I felt a smile begin on my face. How often have I felt that?

I remember the first time I saw Helena. She was standing in my Chemistry class, trying to follow instructions that would light a bunsen burner. I'd never looked at anyone before with lust but that was how I had looked at her. I had imagined throwing her onto my bed and ripping her top across her stomach and over her breasts so that I could put my mouth there, right there on her nipples.

She hadn't seen me. She would see me soon enough but she didn't then and, in my head, I screamed for her to notice me because if she saw me, then I was real.

I would never be real.

I feel like I am a figment of someone else's imagination but I'm real! I have feelings! My heart beats and breaks like everybody else's!

My Helena. My Helena! She can make me real.

I'm thrown out of the cab, my smile becoming a frown and there it is. That tiny voice telling me I am wrong, that everything I have hoped for has gone and I am going to be shut into a corner and kicked to death.

It's not possible. I have shown Nikki I am a force to be reckoned with, even though I am soft. She doesn't have the power to kill me, just as I cannot kill her.

When you lose someone that you hate, you find a strange connection between push and shove. You need and you don't need. You love and you hate. I hated Nikki but I had learned that I loved her, too. When I felt the push of her, I shoved back and when I shoved, she pushed.

We were a symmetry neither understood.

I welcomed the icy, wet rain on my face, back to the cold I was used to. I am a creature of habit and I hadn't liked being away from my flat. It was the four walls I felt safe in. The safety of four walls is often underestimated but not me, I knew where I couldn't be hurt.

I pushed the front door to the building, my rucksack catching as the door swung shut behind me.

"Fuck sake," I muttered, shifting my shoulder to unsnag it and I walked to Freya's door, trying to hide a smile as I knocked.

I remembered the night I had stood there with four cans of lager in my hand, Ethel so pleased that I had finally agreed to have dinner with my attractive Norwegian neighbour, and that same shiver of excitement ran through me, fireworks of memory. I felt myself waiting.

And waiting...

And then the smile faded because I knew my feeling that things were wrong were more than just a feeling. I began to bang my fists on Freya's door, all the while thinking, 'No, Nikki wouldn't come here. She wouldn't leave her comfort zone.'

Would she?

Would I leave the safety of my four walls?

"Fuck!" I shouted, running up the stairs, shrugging off my rucksack, finding my door ajar. I stopped. What had she done? Could she have hurt Freya?

Could *she?*

Could I have hurt Ness?

It was like talking to a mirror, I realised, my heart sinking with all the fear I could feel. And that was a lot of fear. Every fear was in opening my door, not knowing what I might see.

How can I go on? I have no choice, like everybody else. I go on because I am real. Because every emotion inside of me is as real as the next person's and my loves and hates are just as powerful as the next woman's. Every time my heart beats, someone else's heart beats somewhere else.

And as I push open the door to my flat, the four walls that have held me together for so long, through every heartache and anguish anyone could imagine, find me.

I can hear Joy Division on the radio with Ian Curtis telling me that "Love will tear us apart again".

I step forward, every second in slow motion, as the door edges back revealing the scene in my safe haven.

There is no scream left in me.

My eyes fall straight in front of me to my bed where my nemesis lies, her fucking killer blue eyes tightly shut, a smug smile on her sleeping face. Nikki is lying next to Freya, *my* Freya. Why is *my* Freya in a bed next to Nikki?

I feel a heartbeat begin to choke in my throat.

And then I turn my head to the left and see Helena lying on my wooden floors, a stagnant pool of dark, red blood that has made its way from her stomach surrounding her.

I don't even realise I am crying as I run to her, throwing myself to my knees, my jeans soaking in the blood as I skid towards her.

"No! No, baby! No!" I scream, in my tears and in my broken heart and with every single fear alive.

Helena is lying still, staring at my ceiling. But her face has been bashed in, the bruises long set. I hold her once pretty face in my hands, kissing her, to bring her back to life.

Like the cold of Scottish rain, I know the cold of her blood and I whimper as I cradle her. My poor baby is dead. How could this have happened? Why would she be here?

I laid her head back on the floor, closing her eyes, droplets of my tears wetting her face. I'd never see her smile again. I'd never feel the joy from that cheeky wink she'd give me. Her warm arms would never find their way around me.

But more than that, I lost the hope for a future. A future where we might have been together and lived happily ever after with the dead child in her stomach. I could have loved that baby. I could have loved Helena forever. We could have been a family.

I could've, I could've...I turned my head and only then did I notice the tiny cut on Freya's head. Freya, who was in bed with Nikki.

Nothing was making sense. I felt the hysteria build in my chest as I began to hum, standing up from Helena not knowing what I should do or where I should be or what I should be feeling. Helena was dead and there was nothing I could do to save her. There was no forward wind for our love to sail us forward.

But Freya? We might've had a chance.

If I want to hate Nikki, I have to love Nikki, I have to *feel* Nikki.

I took the deep breaths I needed to calm the horror of anxiety that might overtake me. Please let me have four safe walls!

I am Nikki. What am I going to do? I've seen Ness in blood and I've known I could've been ended. I'm Nikki, what do I do?

I do what I would do because I *am* Nikki. I'd get on a plane and I'd kill the thing I loved the most — Helena — and then I'd try to fuck up whatever love I might've had with Freya.

My feet had worked their way to Freya's side of the bed. I put my fingers to her neck, feeling the beat of blood pulsing through her. I had to save her, so I got my hands under her armpits and I dragged her, not caring about the bruises she might have as I bounced her down the stairs to her flat. Away from us, she was safe.

Her keys had been lying in a pile where her clothes were and I had managed to get everything back into Freya's flat without anyone noticing. I had lain her on top of her bed, kissing her, knowing she would wake up soon, never knowing I had been back and hoping it stayed that way.

I went back to my flat, closing the door and locking it from the inside. I looked again at Helena. I had fallen in love with her as a child really and now, as an adult, I didn't love her any less but I didn't love her any more.

Love was a constant that I had no control over.

It didn't stop my heart from breaking. A love lost will always bring a heart to breaking point. It's how you cope that determines the outcome of your love.

There was a naked woman in my bed and her name was Nikki.

There was a naked woman in my bed and her name was Nick.

Who would kill who?

I had to kill Nikki because she killed Helena because I killed Ness. And if Helena was dead, I had to die. It was clear and unclear.

The difference is that there is no difference.

CHAPTER FIFTEEN

The corridors shone white, the brilliant walls and ceilings interrupted only by a stray streak of sunshine that dared puncture the sterility with heat. A faint clip-clop could be heard in the distance, growing louder as the seconds ticked by, introducing footsteps marching in tandem to a destination marked as 'Number Forty-Seven' on a door. The footsteps ceased and silence crept in once more but in these corridors of brilliant white, a silence never lasted for long.

There was a man, a doctor, obvious in his white lab coat and clipboard. His thick glasses lay heavy on the bridge of his nose and every night when he got in bed, finally removing them, he'd have a dent where they had sat. But he didn't care. His nose was the least of his worries.

He tapped his clipboard with his pen, getting the attention of his students as planned, before clearing his throat to speak.

"This here is Nicola X," he said, pointing his favourite pen at number forty-seven's door. "Who can tell me about her?" he asked the eager to impress students of psychiatry.

Every one of the six raised their hands in the air, desperate to show their superior how much they had learned.

Dr Hunter pushed his glasses up his nose to focus and chose Tina because she looked like his ex-wife, when she was younger and thinner and still loved him. He blinked, seeing a softness in her lips that reminded him of days gone when his wife would have let him kiss her.

"You," he said, gruffly.

"Patient's name is Nicola X. She was admitted approximately eleven months ago following a complete mental breakdown. Currently she exhibits the symptoms of multiple personality disorder with bipolar disorder and a bit of anxiety thrown in for good measure," Tina reeled off, proud of her extensive knowledge of the patient.

Dr Hunter nodded. "Tell me about her alternate personalities." Maybe he would ask Tina out for a drink.

Tina smiled up at Dr Hunter. She was twenty-four and in awe of the older man showing her favouritism. These tight tops had worked to her advantage, she thought, making her degree irrelevant. They looked at her chest before they looked at her accomplishments.

"When Nicola was admitted, she was exhibiting signs of an alternative personality that did not fit with the description from her mother. Nicola was insistent her name was Nick. She spoke this in a thick, Scottish accent, despite having lived here in Birmingham her entire life. She claimed at that point that Nick was being terrorised but wouldn't go into details about this.

The following day, when I spoke to her, she said (this time in an American accent) that her name was Nikki and she had no idea why she was here, that she had a painting to finish and a date that she'd like to make and could she please be let out. She was pleasant, non-obstructive and seemingly had no knowledge of prior events leading to her hospitalisation."

"Very good, Tina," Dr Hunter smiled. He was definitely going to ask her out.

*** *** ***

They tell me my name is Nicola. They tell me lots of things but they don't know the whole story. They only ever see a third.

I am Nicola and I am Nikki and I am Nick. And I will tell you why.

When I was a little girl, I lived with my mother and father and I did everything that normal little girls do, except I knew I wasn't a normal little girl because I had friends that no-one else could see or hear.

These friends would whisper to me, like an angel and devil on each shoulder, as I would nod and listen to them.

As I grew older, the voices grew quieter and I knew then that my friends had left me. Teenagers are not known for their patience and I was no different. I had plenty of real friends, who would come to my bedroom and listen to music. My best friend was called Nina and she would bring her David Bowie and the Flaming Lips albums to my house, with a bag of crisps for us to share. We would laugh, lying back on my bed listening to our favourite songs over and over again. Nina told me that she wanted to drive a motorbike across the sandy, desert roads of Oklahoma, feeling the heat on her leather-clad legs as the engine drowned out all other sounds.

"Why?" I asked, thinking how pretty her face was. I could've lifted a pencil to sketch her if I'd had the courage then to ask.

Nina felt like a guiding light across the desert of my life then, her bravery and strength finding an envy inside me that made my heart tremble with jealousy. I wanted what Nina had: that carefree life, that ability to throw off worries, the freedom to be who I wanted to be.

I knew I'd never have that. I could hear the bells tolling in my ears, ringing like memories. I would never have it unless I…unless I…split myself.

I could be happy. I could be successful.

I could be sad. I could be unrealised.

I could experience every emotion and yet none could touch me.

I could hold a pencil in my hand and draw the face of the woman I loved, if I could take my heart and understand that there would be more than one woman in it.

I began to laugh. If only I could take a woman and she could realise I had more than one heart. How to tell?

Nina took my hand, and in taking my hand, she touched me right through to my heart. A touch can carry weight when it's beginning is anchored in love.

Her eyes were all I needed to fall in love. Isn't that how you fall in love? By staring at the monster who has possessed you? Every lover is a monster out there to take control of your love. And the only difference between you and me is that I know the monsters who are inside me. I can see them and love them.

But more than that, I let them live.

My girl, Nina, she would stand and wait for my arms to envelope her. She came to me with her arms open and invited me in. For months, we were as happy as two women together can be until the problems found a way in.

When Nina turned her arms from me, I turned my mind from her because I don't understand how to love someone with all of my mind. But part of my mind? I can do that.

Nina didn't stay. I looked at my face in the mirror, seeing the pain I was left with and knew I needed another love.

I needed love.

Here in my mind I felt love tear me apart. I shut it down and I opened it back up. A mind inside a head is all about the thoughts and dreams and memories. I made them all for Nikki and for Nick.

There came a day when I could not bear the pain of being without Nina anymore. I had taken a razor blade to my thigh and watched as the blood had run down my leg, feeling nothing.

I had to make myself feel something but my heart was dead. Without Nina, I was nothing, I felt nothing.

Nina. Malena. Helena.

Love unsure. Love. Love gone. Love come back.

From Nina, a woman I had grown to love, were women in my head growing for me to make love. I was seeing that I could have Nina in so many different ways.

I could meet her as the love of my life, after a succession of relationships, where I would have to find myself through briefly loving others. You have to know love to know when it is real and large.

I could love her as a child, through my teens into the life I had now, where years were magic numbers that I had to imagine in my mind.

I had to imagine it all in my mind.

My mind is a world where families could grow, loves could be found and dreams could be realised.

As soon as I shut my eyes, it was all there.

*** *** ***

Dr Hunter smiled at Tina before her spoke. "Have you been talking to it?"

Tina felt her smile falter as she heard her patient referred to as "it". She had grown attached to Nicola X, from weeks of trying to interact and her silent observation.

"Nicola is a highly intelligent individual. She's just traumatised. I believe if we can remove or reduce the trauma, her fractured mind will gather itself, adjust and like a jigsaw will piece itself together," Tina said.

Dr Hunter chuckled and Tina saw then the arrogance in his gritted smile. He was a man who had never been happy around women, a man who used his fragile power to get the upper hand because he was a scared little boy beyond the title he hid behind.

"And how will it piece itself together?" Dr Hunter asked.

"With love," Tina said, quietly, hating herself for speak the truth and loving herself for being able to.

Dr Hunter looked at Tina, his eyes lingering a moment longer on her chest than they should have. "Would you like to come out tonight for a drink with me?" he smiled.

Tina smiled back, playing the game of medical politics, answering, "I'm sorry. I have a date tonight."

She found a perverse pleasure in seeing Dr Hunter's face fall when he had been so sure of her agreeing.

"Of course," he said, regally, sweeping his hand across his clipboard, like Tina meant nothing. Because, to him, she really did mean nothing.

Tina smiled.

*** *** ***

The moon was full and bright. White and large and speaking hope in its purity. The light it gave off guided the footsteps of those who trod in the dark of corridors that blinked white when the sun had its time.

There was the rattle of fake lights, a poor man's path to an enlightenment that would never come. You could smell the disappointment as you walked the corridors in the hospital, rooms separated by nothing more than bricks that made up walls.

There was no competition to the bricks inside the minds of patients that made walls no man could penetrate.

No man.

But maybe a woman?

Tina crept along the corridors she knew so well, having done so every night for months, watching her step as she tip-toed her dance to the paths that seemed so loud during the day. How could darkness quieten her feet?

In the black of night, is the only sound that a lover hears the beat of their heart's desire?

At the door of 'Number Forty-Seven', Tina stopped her steps, looking left and right, before she slipped her key in the lock of the door.

As she shut the door behind her to watch Nicola X, she was ignored. Nicola X ignored her because she was in her world. A world that Tina didn't yet fit into.

Tina whispered, "Nicola, it's me," as she sat down at the end of Nicola's bed. Tina sat here every night and Nicola ignored her every night but Tina was confident her persistence would win through.

Nicola sat on her bed, staring, talking to someone who wasn't there.

Tina held her hand. She could wait. Anything good in life was worth waiting for. Tina knew she shouldn't feel connected to a patient but there was something different here, a movement, a turn of the head from Nicola that had hit her in her guts.

Where does love begin and end?

Is it the drop of an eyebrow or a harsh word spoken in defence? Who knows the magic unless you are a magician, a skilled manipulator of a heart that can contain a tiny bit of love, waiting to find the one who will ignite you?

A magician or a doctor who has studied for months to find the specimen for their thesis and who has crept in during the quiet nights to sit with a patient no one else could engage with.

A little under a year ago, Tina had been delighted to start work in the hospital after requesting to be placed there. She had followed the story of Nicola X in the newspapers and had been inextricably attracted, her common sense over-riding her attraction by telling herself it was the academics of Nicola's mind that interested her.

Tina began slowly. Every love begins slowly. Every hatred begins slowly. Sometimes there is no way of knowing whether it is love or hate that is beginning. There is little to separate love from hate, little to separate a love from a love…from one woman to another…from a Malena to a Helena…from a Nina to a Tina. Where do insanity and reality meet? They meet in hearts split by love.

Tina sat in the corner of Nicola's room and she watched, listening to the heartache that was spoken in Nicola's words. Tina saw a lot more than she had let on to Dr Hunter. Inside of Tina, there were a million stories that needed to be told.

Inside of Nicola, a million stories were telling themselves in her mind. What separates one mind from another when love can bond them?

Tina crept into the room of Nicola, almost a year since their first meeting and Tina waited, knowing the signs.

At midnight, Nicola would move from Nick's Scottish accent to Nikki's American one, her manner would jump from misery to optimism. Tina watched it all, her heart soaring and dropping as she found herself falling in love.

"I'll hold your hand every night," Tina told Nicola.

Nicola squeezed her hand.

"I'll never let go," Tina whispered.

*** *** ***

What comes first? The joy of love or the broken heart? Who is the lover and who has the broken heart? In life, you take a smile from another and you try to own it, to pretend that smile is for you but it's always for them. The lover comes before the love.

That stupid heart that beats and breaks is a betrayal you'll never stop because when your heart looks, it gives itself away, and there's no coming back from where your heart has turned its stupid eyes.

Every love is stupid.

Every lover is filled with stupidity. Their heart will be broken, their mind will be twisted and what they once thought normal, will turn their veins cold with terror.

Every love is a terror.

*** *** ***

When I close my eyes, I am Nikki.

When I open my eyes, I am Nick.

In between, I am forced to be Nicola.

I have love and hate in the palms of my imaginary hands. I'll never let this go because I'll never be unhappy but I'll never be fulfilled. There are only simple moments when I open my eyes and I can see everything. Every turn in my life that has lead me here, I can see. I can see every turn that has taken Nikki to find her love in Malena. I can see the road that Nick needs to walk down to find Helena again.

I hate them all. They make my heart break. Every fucking woman I have loved has taken my heart and thrown it into a shredder, while I stood and watched.

I have given them all me and they've taken me. Where am I?

Who will love me?

*** *** ***

The door opens slowly on number forty-seven's room. There is a girl on the bed, her knees held up to her chest, wearing white loose trousers and a short-sleeved white shirt. She is staring ahead, as she rocks gently, mumbling to herself in the padded cell.

"It's me again," Tina tells her.

Angela Peach is the author of *47*, *The Blurring*, *In Reflection*, *Playing My Love*, *A Darker Kind of Love* and a short story collection, *Chill*. Her next novel, *Rhythm in my Heart* is due to be published later in 2018.

You can contact Angela at:

Facebook — facebook.com/Angela-Peach
Twitter — @angelapeach1
Website — www.angelapeach1.com

S J Campbell is the author of *Violet's Story*, *The Knowing*, *Diary of a Broken Heart*, *The Strange Adventures of Mavis Street*, *Ishinnie* and a short story collection, *Little Whispers*. His latest novel, currently untitled, is due to be published at the end of the year.

You can contact Scott at:

Facebook — facebook.com/AlbaScott1970
Twitter — @AlbaScott1970
Website — ringe709.wixsite.com/sjcampbell

Both authors also had a story included in the short story collection *L Is For*, released to raise money for the charity R U Coming Out.

If you have enjoyed this book, we ask that you please leave a review on Amazon and thank you for your support.

www.ingramcontent.com/pod-product-compliance
Lightning Source LLC
Chambersburg PA
CBHW052142220626
47052CB00005B/1159